The Worry Week

THE
Worry Week

A NOVEL BY

ANNE LINDBERGH

PICTURES BY

KEVIN HAWKES

DAVID R. GODINE & *Publisher*

BOSTON

Published in 2003 by
DAVID R. GODINE, *Publisher*
Post Office Box 450
Jaffrey, New Hampshire 03452
www.godine.com

LIBRARY OF CONGRESS CATALOGING-IN-PUBLICATION DATA
Lindbergh, Anne
The Worry Week
Summary: Left alone for a week in their family's
summer house on a Maine island, Allegra and
her two sisters scrounge for food and search
for the treasure supposedly hidden
somewhere on the premises.
1. Children's stories, American. [1. Sisters—Fiction.
2. Buried treasure—Fiction. 3. Maine—Fiction]
1. Hewitt, Kathryn, ill. II. Title.

PZ7.L6572Wo 1985 [Fic] 84-19299
ISBN 1-57692-239-2

FIRST EDITION 2003
Printed in the United States of America

For Saran, 'E', and Ansy,

who would have liked to do the same.

What seas what shores what grey rocks and
what islands
What water lapping the bow
And scent of pine and the woodthrush singing
through the fog
What images return
O my daughter.

T.S. ELIOT – "Marina"

The Worry Week

CHAPTER ONE

There are twelve long months in every year, but we spend only one of them in Maine. As far as I'm concerned, that means that eleven-twelfths of my life are wasted. Alice is too absent-minded to care much where she is, but Minnow agrees. Only July is real for me and Minnow, because July is the month we spend on North Haven Island.

My name is Allegra Sloane, and I'm eleven years old. Alice is my older sister. She's thirteen, going on two – meaning that most of the time, she isn't all there. She wanders around outdoors quoting poetry aloud, and likely as not, she walks straight through a patch of poison ivy. Even then, she doesn't notice anything until she begins to itch. But she's nice.

Minnow is my seven-year-old sister. Her real name is Edith, but we never call her that. She's small for her age and has dark hair, like my mother.

Only my father would insist on naming his three daughters

after girls in a poem without stopping to think that we might turn out to be totally different from the poetry girls. He teaches American literature at a university in Boston, and his specialty is Henry Wadsworth Longfellow. He named us after the girls in Longfellow's poem "The Children's Hour": *Grave Alice, and laughing Allegra, and Edith with golden hair.*

As I said, it didn't turn out that way. Alice got the golden hair. It takes something awfully funny to get a laugh out of me; in fact, my parents say I'm too serious for my age. Minnow is the one who tends to giggle, but she'll outgrow it with time. Since there's not a golden hair on her head, "Edith" just doesn't suit her, and she's "Minnow" to us.

"What would you have done if Minnow had been a boy?" I once asked my father. "You can't call a boy *Edith.*"

My father took the question seriously. "*Henry,*" he said after thinking about it. "Or perhaps *Wadsworth* would be more original."

Wadsworth? I never told Minnow how close she had come to being named Wadsworth. I was afraid she'd scream.

If there's one thing my father likes better than Longfellow, it's Maine, although actually the two are connected in his mind, because of an old family story.

It seems Longfellow taught at Bowdoin College in Maine, and while he was there, my great-great-grandfather was one of his favorite students. My father used to tell us how they even wrote to each other for a while afterward. As a matter of fact, Alice and Minnow and I got a little tired of hearing how Great-great-grandfather Benjamin Sloane knew Henry Wadsworth Longfellow. We were much prouder of the fact that our family built one of the first summer houses on North Haven almost a hundred years ago, and still went back each summer.

Every year since I can remember, we've packed up the car

4

on the first of July and driven to Rockland, where we catch the ferry to North Haven. The drive takes about four and a half hours from Boston, and the ferry ride is seventy minutes, dock to dock. We love every second of it, and we know it all by heart. Sometimes in winter, when we're bored, we shut our eyes and rehearse.

"Now Mother says, *For God's sake, don't take that wrong turn for Augusta!*" Alice will say.

I yell, "There's the bridge at Bath! But we didn't make it through the traffic light."

Then Minnow chips in, "Seventeen minutes left to catch the ferry. And I need to pee!" Minnow has quite an imagination for a seven-year-old.

After we reach the island, something happens to us all. It's as if we get salt water instead of blood in our veins. Everyone relaxes, and after a few days, no one cares what time it is or when meals are going to be. Even my father forgets to check the mailbox for letters from the university.

The mailbox is a mile up the road, and there are a million mosquitoes on the way. We always walk there because once we're on the island, we don't use the car except for buying groceries, and we don't even do that until we have to. My mother hates going into the village. There's only one grocery store, and you meet everyone on the island in it, fighting over the last box of Cheerios. My mother is like me; she wants to pretend we're the only people around.

"Why can't we live here all year?" I used to ask. "I hate coming just when all the summer people come."

"Maybe someday, when I retire," my father would say. "This house isn't weatherproof anymore – it needs a lot of work before anyone could survive a winter in it. Why don't you girls hunt out the treasure? Then maybe we could afford a few repairs."

That treasure was another old family story, only it wasn't based on fact like the one about Longfellow. It was based on rumor. My father had an uncle in a nursing home in Boston who used to tell us there was something valuable in our house on North Haven. He never said what it was – in fact, we suspected he didn't know himself. But he insisted that way back in 1891 when the house was built, a treasure had been hidden behind some secret panel. Although I took the story with a grain of salt, I used to hunt for the treasure on rainy days. If we ever found it, I told myself, not only could we afford repairs – we could afford to spend all summer in our house instead of renting it to strangers in June and August to make ends meet.

"Why don't you bring your uncle here some July so he can show us where the panel is?" Minnow used to ask my father.

My father would just laugh and say, "Secret panel, my eye! Uncle Benjie isn't well enough to travel, Minnow, and even if he were, I wouldn't want to spoil his story."

Last summer, we were halfway through July when the nursing home telephoned to say that my father's Uncle Benjie had died and my parents were needed back in Boston to make arrangements for the funeral. I was sorry about Uncle Benjie, but I'm ashamed to say I was even sorrier about leaving Maine.

"Right now?" I wailed. "We can't leave in the middle of July! We still have seventeen and a half days of vacation left!"

I try not to count because vacations are better when you forget what day it is, but something in my head keeps tab in spite of myself. I'm a tab-keeping sort of person.

"You girls won't be leaving Maine," my father said. "We're sending you to Aunt Ruth, over in Belfast. It's only for a week. We'll all come back next Thursday night and have another ten days together on the island."

Even Alice, who never listens, looked up when he said this.

6

Aunt Ruth is really our great-aunt, and she has ideas that went out with the Model-T Ford. My parents always send us to her after we leave the island so we can have a little more vacation. We've never been able to convince them that we'd rather go straight home to Boston.

"Please don't send us to Aunt Ruth!" said Alice. "She makes us go to bed at six-thirty."

It's true. Aunt Ruth thinks anyone under the age of twenty-one should go to bed at six-thirty. What's more, we have to eat supper at five, and it's only bread and milk because anything heavier lies on the stomach, according to Aunt Ruth. Whereas what really happens is that we lie on our stomachs, moaning from hunger, until we fall asleep at midnight.

"Aunt Ruth thinks the water in Maine is too cold for swimming," I protested. "She won't let us go barefoot, and she makes us wear hats to church on Sundays."

"A fate worse than death!" my father said.

Minnow looked up from her project, which was using school glue to cover coffee cans with seashells. You couldn't see the shells for the glue, and it smelled foul, but my parents thought it would curb her artistic temperament if they stopped her. Artistic temperament, my eye! She just likes to get her fingers in the glue so she can lick them. Minnow is a glutton for school glue.

"I won't go!" said Minnow. "Aunt Ruth calls me Edith."

"And she makes us wear dresses to meals," I added.

My father exploded. Thinking back, I suppose he didn't want to leave the island any more than we did. We weren't making it any easier for him.

"Nonsense!" he said. "A little discipline won't hurt you for once. You've been running around like a bunch of savages."

"Let's just hope Aunt Ruth can take them on such short

notice," my mother said. "I'll call her right now." Then she sighed. "I suppose I'd better call Dickie Moon while I'm at it and tell her she doesn't need to come when we're away."

Dickie Moon is a lobsterman's wife who lives on the island. She keeps an eye on our house during the winter, and in summertime she comes to clean. When we were really little, she helped my mother keep an eye on us, so now she considers herself part of the family. We all love Dickie except for one thing: She's easily offended. She's always misinterpreting what we say, and if we don't keep her posted on every single thing that goes on in our lives, her feelings get hurt. I knew my mother's sigh was because the phone call to Dickie would take three times as long as the one to Aunt Ruth.

While my mother was being tactful with Dickie Moon, my father hurried off to check the hot water heater, and the toilet that won't stop flushing, and the place in the attic where the rain dribbles in if there's a storm. As for the rest of us, we tore through the house throwing things into suitcases because my parents wanted to leave the next day on the early-morning ferry.

Minnow filled a shopping bag with shells and school glue, and Alice wrapped up some pepperoni sausage in case Aunt Ruth starved her to death. For all she's so golden-haired and poetic, Alice has a sordid mania for sausage. She likes it hot. I thought it inconsiderate of her to choose pepperoni because it's too hot for me and Minnow. Of course, Minnow could survive for a week on school glue, but what about me?

My mother came away from the phone looking worried. "Aunt Ruth says she can't meet the girls on the morning ferry. She wants us to come on the noon boat instead."

"We've already got reservations on the morning ferry," said my father. "Can't the girls wait for her in Rockland?"

Minnow's face lit up. "We can go to the five-and-dime!"

My mother looked doubtful. "Alone in Rockland? Aunt Ruth would be horrified!"

"Alice is thirteen," my father reminded her. "Call back and explain, and then let's walk on the beach. It's low tide."

He slipped out of the room before my mother had a chance to ask him why he didn't call back himself. Both my parents are a little intimidated by Aunt Ruth.

I slumped down on the kitchen doorstep, feeling sorry for myself. Although Alice and Minnow had complained about Aunt Ruth, I could tell they didn't mind leaving the island as much as I did. And my parents were making arrangements without consulting me, as if my opinion didn't count. I could hear my mother's voice patiently trying to convince Aunt Ruth that Alice was plenty old enough to look after us in Rockland.

Then my father appeared in the doorway, carrying a fishing net. No one who saw the eager look on his face would guess that his hours on the island were numbered.

"How's my laughing Allegra?" he teased.

My father loves the beach at low tide because of the things he finds: crabs, and mussels, and funny kinds of snails. My mother is just the opposite. She says that if you look for little things down by your feet, you miss the glory of the shore. She likes to walk fast, with her chin up and her hair flying out behind.

I agree with my mother in principle, but I can't resist looking down anyway. That summer, I was hunting for sand dollars, and Minnow was collecting shells for her project. As for Alice, she would pick up anything that had a hole in it and wear it on a string around her neck. Once she even wore a sea urchin that hadn't lost its spines. It gave her a rash, but she ignored it.

Anyway, that day we were anxious to get down to the beach because we all more or less felt it was our last day of freedom. All except Minnow, that is.

"I have to finish my coffee can," she said. "If I take it to Aunt Ruth's, the shells will fall off on the way."

We had been only two weeks on the island, and Minnow had covered five coffee cans with foul-smelling shells. But as I said, my parents didn't dare stop her.

"Are you sure you'll be all right by yourself?" my mother asked. "We won't be gone more than an hour."

Minnow said she was sure. She was already licking the glue from her fingers with a greedy look on her face. It was disgusting.

The rest of us walked down the path to the shore, picking wild raspberries and swatting at the mosquitoes.

"How do mosquitoes survive when we go away?" I wondered. "We're only here for one month of the year. What do they eat the rest of the time?"

Nobody answered. My mother and father were making plans for their trip to Boston, and Alice was quoting Shakespeare. Her school was producing *Romeo and Juliet* that coming fall, and Alice had the part of Juliet. I know we should have been happy that she was so talented and all, but the truth is, she was driving us crazy.

"*O Romeo, Romeo! wherefore art thou Romeo?*
Deny thy father, and refuse thy – Damn!*"

The rest of us were following the path around a patch of thistles. Alice walked straight through.

"I've never heard of anyone refusing a damn before," I said. "Do you suppose that's because no one ever gives a damn?"

"Very funny," said Alice, rubbing her legs. She was wearing shorts.

"I hope you're wearing a long dress for this part," I said. "If

Romeo sees your legs the way they look now, he'll have a purple fit on stage."

But Alice was already reciting again. That's one good thing about Alice: She hardly ever gets mad. She's the sweetest tempered person I know, and she's too lazy to bear a grudge.

"*What's Montague?*" she demanded, flinging her arm out dramatically and hitting my father right in the stomach.

"*It is nor hand, nor foot,*
nor arm, nor face, nor any other part
Belonging to a man – "

My father groaned. "Alice, do you mind? And watch out for the hornets' nest over there on your right!"

We walked along the low-water line, following the curve of the beach. My father gathered some periwinkles in a plastic margarine dish that had been washed up with the tide. He wanted to cook them for supper, but my mother made him throw them back.

"We have to finish up the stew tonight," she told him.

I found nine more sand dollars, and eight of them were perfect. The ninth had a hole in it. I gave it to Alice to wear around her neck.

"Thanks, Legs!" said Alice.

She calls me *Legs* when she's feeling particularly fond of me. My father disapproves. He says Longfellow would turn over in his grave if he could hear her.

My mother hates most of the stuff that the tide brings in. She says in her time it was only driftwood, never plastic. But I like the plastic too: dishes and bottles and things that come in handy. Once I found a doll with just the legs missing. I gave it to Minnow, and she has refused to go to bed without it ever since.

"Here's a shoe!" I said. "I wonder who it belonged to?"

Alice looked at it soulfully.

"What's in a name? That which we call a shoe
By any other name would smell as sweet.
So Romeo would – "

"That's enough, Alice!" my father said sharply. "Let's keep Shakespeare off the beach."

Alice just smiled and threaded her sand dollar on a really disgusting piece of cord she found that was jumping with sand fleas. *"So Romeo would, were he not Romeo called – "* she continued.

"Don't put that filthy thing around your neck!" I warned her.

"I won't," said Alice, and then she did.

There was blood running down one leg where she had bumped into some barnacles. I splashed salt water on it. She didn't even notice, although it must have stung. It's a good thing I'm around to take care of Alice.

Suddenly, my father stopped and turned toward my mother with a wistful look on his face. "We're going to be in a hot, noisy city for the next week," he reminded her. "I think I would like periwinkles for supper. Does it matter about the stew?"

My mother said that the rest of us would eat the stew. She sat down on a rock to wait while he filled his margarine dish again. I was getting a little bored and remembered that I hadn't packed any books. When you have to go to bed at six-thirty, you do a lot of reading.

"Come on, Alice!" I said. "Let's go back to the house."

Alice followed me, murmuring, *"Were he not Romeo called*
. . . not Romeo called . . ." She was stuck again.

Minnow was sitting on the kitchen floor, surrounded by shells. She had finished all but the last inch of her coffee can, and there were white smudges around her mouth.

"Hello, brat! What's new?" I asked her.

"Nothing," said Minnow. "Aunt Ruth called, that's all."

I groaned. "What for?"

Minnow shrugged. "Just to talk. She asked if I was being a good girl, the way she always does. Oh, and she said we can't come after all."

"Can't come? What do you mean?" asked Alice.

She got a telegram from a friend of hers in Quebec," said Minnow. "She fell down and broke her hip. The friend, I mean not Aunt Ruth. Aunt Ruth is going up to nurse her."

It struck me that my life was being arranged entirely according to a series of catastrophes that happened to other people. "What about us?" I demanded. "Where do we go?"

"I don't know," said Minnow. "Aunt Ruth wants Mummy to call her back as soon as she gets in. She's in a hurry. Aunt Ruth is, I mean, not Mummy. She has to leave for the airport."

"Terrific!" cried Alice. "We've been saved from a fate worse than death!"

"I'm not sure," I said slowly. "That means we'll be dragged off to Boston, and we'll have to sit around in the heat for a week before we can come back."

I could see by Alice's face that she was trying to choose the lesser of two evils. "Maybe we could go to Belfast anyway," she suggested. "Mrs. Pitts could take care of us."

Mrs. Pitts is Aunt Ruth's housekeeper. She lives in, and she's easier to get along with than Aunt Ruth.

"Mrs. Pitts is going to Quebec, too," said Minnow. "Aunt Ruth said the house would be empty. Maybe we could stay there all by ourselves!" She put a gluey finger into her mouth and giggled.

"We've got our own empty house," said Alice. "Let's just stay here."

I was looking at them and wondering how I ended up with

two feebleminded sisters when suddenly an idea came to me – an absolutely wild, terrifying, glorious idea. Without a word to Alice and Minnow, I ran to the phone and dialed Aunt Ruth's number.

"Hello? Aunt Ruth? This is Allegra Sloane!" I shouted. Aunt Ruth is a little hard-of-hearing. "Yes, Minnow told me. I'm sorry, I mean Edith. No, Mummy isn't back from the beach yet. Yes, I know you're leaving for the airport, Aunt Ruth. That's why I'm calling. I just wanted to say it's all right. We're going to Boston with Mummy and Daddy."

Alice and Minnow crept up to the phone. They stared at me as if I had gone stark, raving mad. I motioned to them to keep quiet.

"Yes, I said *Boston!*" I shouted. "Daddy decided we should go anyway, even before you called, so it's all arranged. *I said it's all arranged!*"

"But, Allegra, I don't *want* to go to Boston!" said Minnow.

"Shut up!" I hissed. "You won't have to."

"Yes, Aunt Ruth!" I shouted into the receiver. "Yes, I'll tell them. I'll give them your message. Have a good trip! Alice sends her love, and so does Minnow. I'm sorry, I mean Edith!"

I hung up the phone and turned around in time to see Alice and Minnow making rude faces. I was about to explain my plan, but just then my parents came back from the beach.

"Don't say a word!" I warned my sisters. "Keep quiet, and let me do the talking."

My mother walked into the kitchen shaking her hair like a dog coming out of the water. She always does that when she comes in from the fresh air. My father put his periwinkles into the sink.

"Did anyone call?" he asked.

Minnow sucked her finger and stared at me. Alice looked

dazed. There was a moment of tension while they waited for me to answer.

"No," I said calmly. "Nobody called."

"Let's finish up the packing and have supper early, then," said my mother. "We have a big day tomorrow."

I grabbed Minnow's hand and pulled her out of the room before she could say something to give away our secret. "Come on, Edith! We'd better practice your real name so you don't faint when Aunt Ruth calls you by it."

We were halfway upstairs when the truth dawned on Minnow. "But, Allegra," she asked, "how can Aunt Ruth call me Edith if she's in Quebec?"

Luckily, my parents were out of hearing.

Alice followed us upstairs, still looking dazed. Her lips were barely moving as she muttered, "*Were he not Romeo called... not Romeo called...* If Aunt Ruth isn't going to meet us, what do we do once we get to Rockland, Legs?"

"Take the ferry right back here again, of course," I said as I tossed a couple of Nancy Drews into my suitcase.

Alice's mouth dropped open. "How can we do that? We don't even have return tickets!"

"We won't need tickets, dummy!" I explained. It takes a while sometimes to get an idea through to Alice. "We're going to stay on the boat. Mummy and Daddy will drive up the ramp, and they'll think we're walking off, but we won't. We'll stow away in the ladies' room."

This was smart planning, and sure to work. The man on shore at the top of the ramp is the one who checks your tickets. The men on the boat are only concerned with getting the cars off fast because the morning ferry turns right around and heads back to North Haven again. As for my parents, they would be in such a hurry that they weren't likely to stop and watch us walk up the ramp. But did my sisters appreciate my brilliant brain work? Fat chance. Instead, they complained.

"That means we can't go to the five-and-dime!" Minnow wailed. Her face crumpled up, and I could see she was going to cry.

"Listen, Minnow!" I said. "Which is more important – to go to the five-and-dime, or to come back to the island?"

"To come back here," said Minnow. She cheered up immediately.

"But, Legs," said Alice, "if we're coming straight back here again, why are you packing those books?"

Alice is enough to try the patience of a saint.

"We've got to make this look true," I told her. "It has to be so real that we believe it ourselves. That way Mummy and Daddy won't suspect anything. But once we're back here, we can relax. Just think – we'll be on the island, and we won't have a worry in the world!"

CHAPTER TWO

W̲e woke up very early the next morning. My father wanted to be at the dock by seven-thirty. There was only time for cold cereal and milk, so we were all a little crotchety and stepping on each other's toes. Besides, my mother made us dress up in skirts and school shoes to impress Aunt Ruth. My school shoes were too tight, and my skirt was too short. I grow by spurts, and I must have had a spurt in July.

"I can't wear this," I objected. "You can see my underpants when I lean over."

"So don't lean over!" my mother snapped.

Then she softened. "Sorry, Allegra. I hate leaving, too, but we'll just have to make the best of it. And that reminds me – I'm counting on you to make sure nothing goes wrong in Rockland this morning. Alice may be older, but if you don't keep an eye on her, she'll wander off the dock and drown."

Alice wandered into the room at that moment, still wearing her pajama bottoms under her skirt. Minnow trailed after her, hugging a shopping bag full of shells and school glue.

My mother sighed and ran her fingers through her hair the way she does when she gets frazzled. "Alice, if you'll look in the mirror, you'll find you've forgotten something. And, Minnow, sweetie, there's no way you can manage that bag. It's just one more thing to carry, and you're overloaded as it is."

Ordinarily, Minnow would have made a scene. Instead, she looked relieved and trotted back upstairs to leave the bag in her room. That's when I thought the show was over. Both my parents looked suspicious, but I saved the day.

"Aunt Ruth never lets Minnow use school glue, anyway," I said. "She read somewhere that you can get high, sniffing glue."

We caught the ferry in plenty of time. When it pulled away from the dock and moved into the bay through the early morning fog, it struck me that in seventy minutes, we would be on our own. I was so excited that I had to pinch myself to keep from looking too happy.

"We're supposed to be going to Aunt Ruth's, remember?" I hissed at my sisters. "Cheer down! Look a little sulky!"

Alice stood in the bow of the ferry, clasping her hands as if she were praying. Her lips were moving, and I could tell she was having a real orgy of Romeo and Juliet. Knowing Alice, she probably hoped that some wildly attractive young man was watching her and thinking, "Who is that beautiful girl with the sensitive look on her face?"

Actually, I heard one of the mates yell, "Keep an eye on that goofy blond kid so she don't fall overboard!"

It was cold, so everybody else, attractive or not, sat in the cabin. Minnow knelt on the bench and gazed out the window with a blissful smile on her face, no matter how hard I pinched her. My parents looked more suspicious than ever.

"Happy, Minnow?" my father asked.

"Of course!" said Minnow. "We're going to the five-and-dime!"

I couldn't tell whether she really believed it or if she was just a good actress. Whichever it was, my parents were convinced.

"Have a good time!" said my mother as the ferry pulled into Rockland and the car motors started up. "Don't forget to eat the sandwiches I made for you! Be sure to be on the dock by one o'clock! Give our love to Aunt Ruth!"

The last thing we heard was my father's voice shouting, "We'll telephone tonight from Boston to make sure you arrived safely!"

My sisters looked horrified, and I have to admit that for a moment, I almost ran after the car and confessed. The telephone was a problem that hadn't occurred to me. But before I made up my mind, the car was several blocks away, and it was too late.

"Don't worry," I said. "We'll think of something."

We waited until they were out of sight before we dashed back into the cabin, hid our suitcases under a bench, and crowded into the ladies' room.

The ladies' room on the North Haven ferry was designed for only one lady. It was a tight squeeze for the three of us, and it wasn't the pleasantest smell in the world, especially when you thought of what we're usually breathing as the boat leaves the mainland. First fishy, harbor smells, and mud if it's low tide. Then just oily, ferry smells, spiced with salt water. As Alice puts it when we rehearse the trip at home in wintertime, "It's our first breath of real Maine."

No real Maine was filtering into the ladies' room. In fact, Minnow held her nose. The only window was tiny, had a film of greasy dust, and looked as if no one had ever opened it. Alice rubbed the glass with a piece of toilet paper and peered out. "We're pulling away from the dock!" she announced.

"You don't have to look to know that," I told her. "You can feel it."

The ferry backs out when it leaves the dock, and then turns around. When you're on deck, the backing and turning is fun, but that morning in the ladies' room, I felt a little peculiar, and Minnow was a delicate shade of green. Alice was the only one who didn't seem to mind. Alice has a stomach like a goat.

"You'd better use the toilet while you have the chance, Minnow," I said.

"I don't need to," said Minnow. "I went before I left."

"We're moving forward again," said Alice. "I can see the breakwater. Let's go sit in the cabin!"

"Someone might recognize us," I warned her.

"So what?" said Alice. "They wouldn't be the same people who saw us ride over."

"If someone recognized us, they might tell Dickie Moon, and she knows we're supposed to be in Belfast," I explained.

Minnow giggled. "Dickie wouldn't get mad at us for staying. She'd just be mad that we didn't let her in on the secret."

Just then, there was a loud knock, and somebody rattled the doorknob. We couldn't stay in the ladies' room forever, so we all filed out. The woman who was trying to get in looked scandalized. Luckily, she didn't know us. In fact, I don't think anybody knew us. I silently thanked my mother for being so unsociable.

Even when we walked off the ferry and up the ramp to the island with our suitcases, no one gave us so much as a second glance. Staring straight ahead, we marched by Franklin Water-

man's grocery store and the marble fountain with the lions'
heads and the little fountains underneath for dogs.

"Wait!" said Minnow. "I need a drink!"

"Not now," I hissed. "We have to get out of here in a hurry.
Besides, you know it will only make you want to go to the
bathroom."

Minnow got down on her hands and knees and drank from
the dogs' fountain. Of all the ways to attract attention! I yanked
her away and dragged her on up the hill, past Mrs. Hopkins's
gift shop, past the post office, past the library. Then Minnow
dropped her suitcase and announced, "I need to pee."

We were in the middle of the village, with not so much as
a bush to hide behind.

"Oh, no, you don't!" I said.

I grabbed her hand and ran. Alice puffed along behind us,
carrying Minnow's suitcase as well as her own. We hurried on
until we were beyond the village houses and found a private
bush for Minnow.

Alice sat down on her suitcase. There were tiny beads of
sweat on her forehead, and she was panting. So was I.

"I have to stop and catch my breath," I told her. "When
you're in a car, you don't realize what a steep hill that is!"

Alice put on her Juliet face and gasped:

"How art thou out of breath when thou hast breath
to say to me that thou art out of breath?"

"Speak for yourself," I told her. "Ready, Minnow? Let's get
moving. We've still got miles to go."

Our house is seven miles from the village, and it's a good
thing, too. Nobody comes out to bother us there. It's the last
house on a dead-end road, and the road turns into a grassy
track after our mailbox. Even people who get lost turn back
before they come anywhere near the house.

"Seven miles!" said Alice. "With suitcases?"

"I think we've done one mile already," I told her. "Maybe two. And Minnow can carry her own bag."

"Minnow's isn't heavy," said Alice. "Mine is. It's all those books you made me take so it would seem real!"

"You only put in one book," I reminded her. "If your suitcase is heavy, it's because of that disgusting pepperoni sausage." I don't know how long it took to reach the house because none of us had watches. All I can say is, even though we stopped to rest every two minutes, it seemed like fourteen miles. The sun was touching the top of the fir trees when we got to our mailbox, with one more mile to go. At every step, my suitcase grew heavier and my feet, squeezed into those tight school shoes, were killing me. But I didn't say anything because by then I was a little unpopular with my sisters.

"You and your big ideas!" Alice said grumpily as she flung down her suitcase. "We could have left all the heavy stuff at home, and no one would have known the difference."

"You're right," Minnow agreed. "I did."

"You did what?" Alice and I asked together.

Minnow opened her suitcase. It was completely empty except for her sandwich. I envied her, but it made me shudder to think what would have happened if my mother had looked inside.

I had forgotten about the sandwiches. "Let's eat lunch!"

"Right here?" asked Alice. "This is such a nowhere place!"

She stood up and opened the mailbox. There was nothing inside. It made me feel lonely.

"It's way past noon," I reminded Alice. "Look how low the sun is – it's probably closer to suppertime. And we still have a mile to go."

We sat on the grass to eat our sandwiches. My mother

makes really good ones, with thick slices of bread, lots of butter, and huge piles of ham, cheese, and lettuce. We were so busy eating that no one talked until Alice stood up, rubbed her stomach, and said,

"Hist! Romeo, hist! O for a falc'ner's voice,
To lure this tassel-gentle back again."

"I beg your pardon?" I said. For a moment, I thought maybe she was suffering from sunstroke.

She continued:

"Bondage is hoarse, and may not speak aloud;
Else would I tear the cave where Echo lies,
And make her airy tongue more hoarse than mine – "

"*Nobody's* airy tongue could be more hoarse than yours," I said, rising stiffly and setting off down the road again. "Why don't you give it a rest, Alice?"

Alice must have been born without whatever part of the brain it is that makes you argue. She just picked up her suitcase and started trudging on up the road.

By now, my feet hurt so much that I took my shoes off and walked on the grassy strip in the middle of the road, keeping an eye out for thistles.

"Look!" said Minnow. "Chanterelles!"

Chanterelles are little orange mushrooms with wrinkly caps, and they smell like apricots. They grow in the woods near our house. My father is crazy about them, but the rest of us never ate more than a nibble, to be polite.

"Let's leave them for Daddy," I said. "Do you remember if there's any more of that leftover stew, Alice?"

Alice looked at me dreamily.

"What if it be a poison which the friar
Subtly hath minister'd to have me dead."

I began to wonder whether I could take a whole week of

Juliet. If Alice didn't kill herself first, that is, by marching off a cliff in the fog chanting, "*O Romeo, Romeo! wherefore art thou Romeo?*" In fact, I was choosing flowers for Alice's funeral when we rounded a corner and came in full view of the house.

"Hey, who closed the shutters?" asked Minnow. "It looks as if nobody lives here!"

She was right. The house looked positively haunted, it was so lonely.

"Dickie Moon must have been by to close up," I said. "Let's hope she stays away from now on. And let's keep the shutters closed, except on the bay side. Then no one can tell we're here even at night."

"Who would come by at night?" Minnow asked innocently.

"Murdering thieves!" said Alice in a scary voice. "Hunting for the hidden treasure."

"Very funny!" I told her. "Why don't you help me find a way to get in, instead of frightening Minnow?"

Dickie Moon had locked the house, but we found a loose shutter on a second-story window. Alice gave me a leg up, and I wriggled into our bedroom, scraping my back on the way. Then I went down and let in the others. It was five o'clock already by the kitchen clock.

"I'm starved," said Alice. "That sandwich wasn't enough. Let's have supper right away."

She threw open the refrigerator door and looked perplexed. "Where's all the food?"

"Don't bother with anything fancy," I told her. "Let's just have the rest of the stew, with bread and butter."

"Bread and butter?" said Alice. "Would you settle for ice cubes dipped in marmalade?"

Looking in over her shoulder, I saw what she meant. The refrigerator was almost empty. "I don't understand! What could have happened?"

Minnow had run upstairs the minute she entered the house. Now she came back to the kitchen, toting her shopping bag full of shells and school glue. "There's a note on the kitchen table," she informed us.

Alice held the note up to the light and read it out loud. "'Dear Mrs. Sloane: Came Fri. A.M. to lock up. Took away any food the mice could get after. Sincerely yours, Dickie Moon.'"

"Mice!" I protested. "How could mice get after a refrigerator? Why, she must have brought a truck to cart everything away!"

"There wasn't that much to cart away," said Minnow. "We even ran out of cornflakes at breakfast. I heard Mummy say we were scraping the bottom of the barrel and we'd have to do a big shopping trip in Rockland next Thursday before we take the ferry."

I groaned. "Now you tell us!"

"It's a good thing I packed that pepperoni," said Alice smugly. "Otherwise, I might have starved."

"It's not too late to starve," I warned her. "We're here for a week, remember? We'd better find all the food in the house so we can ration it out. Go see if there's anything in the storeroom, Minnow, while Alice and I check out the refrigerator."

All that Alice and I could find were two onions, one lemon, marmalade, some sugar, and a lot of ice cubes. As for Minnow, she came back with a box of crackers, some tea bags, and six candle stubs.

"There's oil and vinegar in there, too," she informed me. "But I didn't think we'd want to eat them."

"Did you think we'd want to eat candles?" I asked.

"They were in a coffee can," Minnow explained. "Let's burn them so I can decorate the can."

She had set out her project on the kitchen table, and there was already glue on her face.

I shook my head. "Before we do anything at all, we should call home. Mummy and Daddy must have gotten there ages ago. They're probably trying to call Aunt Ruth right now, and they'll panic when no one answers."

Alice grabbed my arm as I reached for the phone. "Are you out of your mind, Allegra? They'll be furious! They'll make us leave the island!"

"Trust me," I said, and I dialed the number.

It was a while before my father picked up the phone. "Daddy? Is that you?" I asked. "This is Allegra. We're just going out for supper, so I thought I ought to call you first to say we're all right. Give my love to Mummy, okay? And Alice and Minnow say to give theirs, too. We have to go now.... What?... What is it? Can't you tell us now? ... But we might go out tomorrow night, too! ... Oh, well, okay. Bye!"

My sisters looked shocked, and I felt a little scared at my own nerve, but I wasn't about to admit it. "So what's wrong?" I asked them. "I never said where we were, did I? And I never mentioned Aunt Ruth, so it isn't as if it were a lie."

But I could tell by their faces that it counted as a lie all the same. "What about when you said we're going out for supper?" asked Minnow.

"That's what we're going to do right this minute," I said, and grabbing the box of crackers, I ran out the door.

It wasn't my conscience that bothered me so much as the fact that my father had said he would call us back the next evening because he had some exciting news. What was I going to do? Last time I thought I'd come up with a new idea, it just got us deeper and deeper into trouble.

Walking on the beach that evening, we felt a little glum, but none of us wanted to show it. I kept telling the others how lucky we were not to be at Aunt Ruth's.

"We'd be in bed by now," I said.

"After bread and milk!" Alice added, with more enthusiasm than I had ever heard her use before for bread and milk.

"Just think," I said. "We can stay up all night reading books, and we can swim without a suit, and we don't have to make our beds!"

Minnow was stuffing her pockets with periwinkle shells. "I can hunt for the treasure all day long, and I can have supper for breakfast and breakfast for supper," she added.

That brought us back to the food problem. Seven days on one box of crackers didn't sound possible. In fact, we finished the crackers that evening, before going to bed. Crackers and marmalade, by candlelight.

A storm was blowing outside. The shutters rattled, and the wind whistled through the underpinnings of the house. Some kind of strange bird was laughing its head off out in the woods. Maybe an owl.

I took my Nancy Drews out of my suitcase, but I didn't feel like reading. Alice said she was tempted to soak in a hot tub with my mother's bath salts, but she didn't have the energy to go run the water. Even Minnow sat staring sadly at her school glue, as if she were calculating how long it would last. When the crackers were gone, we went to bed.

CHAPTER THREE

The next morning, we had wild strawberries for breakfast. They grow along the road, on the way to the mailbox. We ate our way out and ate our way back, catching the ones we had missed before. They were good, but not very filling.

"How long does it take strawberries to grow?" Alice wondered. "It had better be overnight, or we won't have anything for breakfast tomorrow."

"What about lunch and supper today?" asked Minnow.

It worried me, too. Even if we walked back to the village to get food, we only had the money we were going to spend at the five-and dime in Rockland, which wasn't enough to keep us alive for a week. I didn't think they would let us buy on credit at Waterman's grocery store unless we explained who we were. But if we explained, someone would get upset about our staying in the house alone.

"Let's get organized," I said when we were back in the kitchen. "We should look at this as a challenge. We're going to live off the land for a week. Does anyone have any ideas?"

"Yes," said Minnow. "Today, I'm going to hunt for the treasure all day long."

I glanced out the window. "But you can't, Minnow! Look how sunny it is. You can't stay indoors on a beautiful day like this."

Minnow's face puckered dangerously. "Now you're talking just like Mummy, but last night you said we could do whatever we wanted."

"Oh, for heaven's sake!" I said. "Sure you can, but it has to be within reason. We need food desperately! You can't eat treasure. And if you don't eat, you won't even have the strength to hunt for it."

I picked up a pencil and wrote *Menus* on a sheet of paper.

"All we have are onions," Minnow said sulkily. "Is there anything you can do to onions so they don't taste like onions?"

"Except for throwing them out, there isn't," I told her.

"Oh," said Minnow. "Well, what about scrambled seagull eggs?"

"We should plant a garden," said Alice. "Radishes grow fast." I looked at them pityingly. It seemed astonishing that people as intelligent as my parents should have two out of three children with no brains at all.

"You could starve to death waiting for a radish to grow," I told Alice. "Let's be serious. Daddy is always talking about the wild stuff you can eat around here. Now's the time to remember what it is. You know – roots and berries and things."

"*With baleful weeds and precious-juiced flowers,*" Alice added dreamily. She had that poetic look on her face again, and I could tell she wasn't going to be any help at all.

"O! mighty is the powerful grace that lies
In plants, herbs, stones, and their true qualities – "
"If you want to eat stones, feel free to trot down to the beach and stuff yourself," I said. "And anyway, that's the Friar's part, not Juliet's." I was getting so familiar with the play by then that I was thinking of trying out for understudy.

"How long do you have to boil stones before they get soft?" asked Minnow. She spread her shell collection on the kitchen table and started to choose which ones to paste on the candle coffee can.

The shells inspired me. "Periwinkles," I scribbled. "Wild strawberries, raspberries, chanterelle mushrooms."

"Why don't we collect mussels?" asked Minnow. "It's low tide."

We all love steamed mussels. In fact, mussel days are a ritual for our family. We usually have them the day after we arrive and again the day before we leave. Back home during the winter, we all swear that the next July we'll eat mussels at least twice a week, but it never happens. The reason is, they're a pain to collect, a pain to clean, and even a pain to chew because a lot of them have tiny pearls inside that break your teeth. Still, mussels are good.

"Smart thinking," I told Minnow. "We could survive a whole week on mussels, and then there's the broth."

Alice looked horrified. "Mussel broth is gross, Allegra!"

"So what?" I said. "It's nutritious."

When we got down to the beach, the tide was already coming in, so we had to hurry. The mussel bed is pretty far out, and some days the tide doesn't even get low enough to uncover it. You have to twist the mussels off the rocks they grow on because they attach themselves by a sort of beard. My father taught us not to keep the ones that come off too easily, in case they're dead.

The problem is, the mussels on our beach are covered with barnacles, and so are the rocks they grow on. We always wear plastic sandals to protect our feet, even when we're swimming, but our hands get scratched up, and then they sting in the salt water. I don't mind too much, and Alice doesn't notice that kind of thing anyway, but Minnow can't take it.

"Look!" she whimpered, showing me a bloody thumb. "I need a bandage!"

"It looks worse than it is," I told her. "Wash off the blood, and you'll see. It's only a scratch. Work a little faster, can't you? The tide is coming in!"

But Minnow refused to help anymore. "My shorts are all wet," she complained. "I'm going to take them off and collect periwinkles. Periwinkles don't have barnacles."

Alice and I were bent over double, working like dogs. The water was up to our ankles by then, so it was harder to see the mussels, and our pot was only half full. By the time we filled it to the top, the waves were splashing at our knees, and the sun was beating on our backs.

"Where's Minnow?" I asked.

Alice pointed to the far end of the beach. There was Minnow, stark naked. Actually, she didn't look naked at first. She looked as if she were wearing a white bathing suit because the rest of her was tanned. But when you got up closer, you could see it was just skin.

"Where are your clothes?" I called when we were within shouting distance.

"Look at all the periwinkles I got!" Minnow yelled.

Periwinkles are little snails that you can boil and eat with a pin, if you go in for that kind of thing. My father loves them, and my mother can't stand them. My sisters and I don't mind the taste, but we object on principle because they're so cute, almost like pets, unlike mussels, which have so little personality they might as well be vegetables.

"*Where are your clothes, Minnow!*" I yelled.

"I left them next to you!" Minnow yelled back.

I turned around. The place where we had been was covered by three feet of water, and Minnow's clothes were nowhere to be seen. Then I looked out into Penobscot Bay. There were Minnow's flowered underpants, floating out to sea. The rest must have just sunk to the bottom.

"Oh, Minnow!" I groaned. "Those were your new shorts!"

"And my T-shirt with the crocodile," Minnow said sadly. Then she cheered up. "I wonder who'll find the underpants? Maybe a sailor will pick them up and take them home to his daughter."

"More likely they'll wash up on a beach, and somebody like us will see them and say, *Yuck! How disgusting!*" I told her. "You would have done better to keep track of your underpants and leave those poor little periwinkles alone. Are you really going to eat them?"

"Daddy says they don't have souls," said Minnow. "Besides, they're better than onions."

On the whole, my father isn't a narrow-minded man, but I think he's wrong about periwinkles. Not about eating them – that's no worse than eating chicken or fish – but about the souls. If a dog has a soul, why shouldn't a periwinkle? And I'm sure that dogs have souls.

Anyway, we ate those periwinkles for lunch because we were nowhere near finished cleaning the mussels at noon. All you have to do to periwinkles is rinse them off and cook them in boiling water for five minutes. Then you scoop them out with a pin and dip them into melted butter. We didn't have butter, so I made an oil and vinegar dressing instead. Souls or not, they tasted good.

I looked at Minnow, who was still naked except for her plastic sandals and a bandage on her thumb, eating periwinkles as fast as she could scoop them out, with her nose two inches over her plate. It suddenly dawned on me what my father meant about running around like a bunch of savages.

"What would Longfellow say if he could see you now, Edith with golden hair?" I asked her.

"He'd say he would put me in the round tower of his heart," Minnow mumbled through her mouthful of periwinkles.

Even Minnow knows that poem by heart because my father is forever quoting it at us.

"No, he wouldn't," I said. "He'd say, *You disgusting child, where are your underpants?*"

"I'm not getting dressed until we finish cleaning the mussels," Minnow said calmly. "It's too messy."

We took our empty periwinkle shells outside and threw them into the bushes. Then we got back to work.

It takes us a good two hours to clean the barnacles and pull the beards off the mussels, and then we rinse them several times. By the time we're through, our hands are bleeding, our backs are aching, and we're splattered with barnacles. It's a big mess, so we always do it sitting on the lawn.

We didn't get finished until two o'clock. By then, the tide had come up, so we went back to the beach to swim. The water was icy, but it felt good. Minnow splashed around the way little kids do, getting her hair wet and squealing her head off. Alice and I stayed away from her. We don't like getting our heads wet because our ears ache afterward.

"Guess what?" shouted Minnow. "The water feels warmer without a bathing suit. Try it, you'll see!"

"No, thanks," said Alice. "What if a boat comes by?"

We stayed on the beach all afternoon; there was nothing better to do. The tide had gone pretty far down again before we walked back to the house to cook our mussels.

"Put on your nightgown or something," I said to Minnow. "You're getting on my nerves, running around like that."

"After supper," said Minnow. "Mussels are messy. I don't want to get my nightgown all smelly."

"Let's have supper right away," I said to Alice. "Do you know how we're supposed to cook these things?"

"Mummy steams them," said Alice.

"We know that, pea brain, but how do you steam mussels?"

Alice shrugged.

"This is dumb!" I complained. "What a stupid way to live! All we do is worry about food, and hunt for food, and cook food, and clean up after meals. Then what happens? We're hungry all over again. It's a waste of energy. Where's Mummy's cookbook?"

My mother has a whole shelf full of cookbooks at home, but when she's on the island, all she uses is this old Boston Cooking School cookbook that was printed in 1937 and is so mildewed that you can't turn the pages. When I picked it up, the "Lamb and Mutton" section fell out, and it took me five minutes to find where to put it in again. There was nothing about mussels.

"Maybe people didn't eat mussels in the olden days," said Alice. "Or maybe they ate them raw, like savages."

"You can eat yours raw if you like," I told her. "Look, here's a recipe for steamed clams. That ought to be just about the same."

Alice leaned over my shoulder and read, "Allow one-half

cup hot water to four quarts clams; cover closely, and steam until shells partially open.' That sounds easy!"

"It sounds easy, but it doesn't sound right," I said. "I don't think that's the way Mummy does it at all. Oh, why do people have to eat?"

Minnow was rummaging through a pile of old *National Geographics*. She looked up when I mentioned eating. "I eat because I'm hungry," she said, "and Mummy puts in a clove of garlic and a cup of white wine. I heard her tell Dickie Moon."

"Well, why on earth didn't you say so?" I shouted.

"I just did," said Minnow. She went back to her pile of *Geographics*.

I happened to look at the one she was leafing through, and something caught my attention. "'Foraging for Wild Foods,'" I read. "Hey, that might be useful! Let me see it!"

Minnow handed it over and opened another copy to an article with pictures of a tribe in New Guinea who didn't wear any clothes, just beads and feathers. Minnow stared as if she had never seen a naked body before. I didn't take it away from her, though, because I was too busy reading about wild foods. The trouble was, all I found were things like wild asparagus, which doesn't grow on North Haven, and chanterelles, which we already knew about. But the article gave me an idea.

"Doesn't Daddy have a book about wild food in Maine?" I asked. "Where does he keep it?"

"Up on his bedside table," said Minnow, who knew the answer as usual. "Mummy won't cook from it because she doesn't want to poison us."

"Well, I don't want to starve us, so you'll just have to take your choice," I said, and I ran upstairs to find it.

Meanwhile, Alice cooked the mussels. I should have known better than to let her do it by herself; Alice is too poetic to make a good chef. She gets carried away, and you never know what you might be eating. Sometimes she adds things for reasons that must be literary, because for sure they aren't culinary.

"*Double, double, toil and trouble; fire burn, and cauldron bubble,*" she chanted. That's said by the witches in *Macbeth* – much more suitable parts for Alice, in my opinion.

"*Eye of newt and toe of frog, wool of bat and tongue of dog,*" Alice sang.

I had been taking notes on cattail salad, but that caught my attention. Living off the land is fine, if you have to, but eye of newt is going too far. What's more, a really weird smell was coming from the stove. Whatever it was, it wasn't mussels. It made me feel a little dizzy.

"Hey, Alice! What did you put into that pot?" I asked.

"Gin," said Alice, "and an onion. I couldn't find any garlic, and there was no more wine, but there was half a bottle of gin left."

"How much did you put in?" I asked.

"All of it," said Alice. "The mussels are ready now. Could somebody get out the plates?"

My head was reeling from the fumes of the gin, and I almost fainted while I was reaching for the plates. All I could think of was how mad my parents would be when they got back and found out there was no more gin. They like to have a drink at the end of the day, and you can't buy hard liquor on the island.

I put three plates on the kitchen table, and a large bowl for the broth. Alice scooped out three huge piles of mussels. For once, I could make a pig of myself, but somehow I didn't really want to.

"Alice," I said, "aren't you afraid we'll get drunk?"

"We can't," said Alice. "Mummy says alcohol evaporates as soon as it boils, and only the taste is left."

"But I don't *like* the taste of gin!" Minnow protested, looking sadly at her plate.

"I could do without it, personally," I agreed. "I could do without the onion, too. Why didn't you ask us before you threw all that junk in?"

Alice took a spoonful of broth and held it in her mouth for a long time before she swallowed. "I think maybe I'd better divide up the peppcroni," she said thoughtfully. "That way, I'll be sure it lasts until Mummy and Daddy come home."

"But Minnow and I can't eat pepperoni," I reminded her.

"Pity!" Alice said smugly.

I felt like strangling her. "Of all the dumb tricks you could play on us, this takes the blue ribbon!" I said, choking on my broth. "Think of all the time we wasted preparing the mussels! It was stupid and nasty and inconsiderate of you!"

With anyone else, it would have been the start of a real fight, but fights are impossible with Alice. It isn't that she's meek. She's just sweet-tempered.

"I'm sorry, Legs," she said. "I admit it doesn't taste good. Next time, we can just use water."

"Next time!" I wailed. "Do you think I'm going to spend another day scraping barnacles? My fingers are in shreds! I hope I never see another mussel in my life!"

Nevertheless, we ate those mussels. We were too hungry to pass them up. But we threw out the broth. No matter what my mother says about boiling alcohol, gin is gin. It made me feel sick and sleepy, and I shuddered to think what my mother would say if she knew about it.

That reminded me. "Oh, no! I forgot to call home!"

"Call home again?" asked Alice. "What for?"

"Because Daddy said he'd call us at Aunt Ruth's again tonight," I explained. "He said he has some exciting news."

I dialed the number, a little more sure of myself this time. Of course, it was embarrassing when my father asked to talk to Aunt Ruth, but I said she was out of the house, which was true if you came right down to it. In any case, he was more interested in telling me his news, and when I heard what it was, I nearly dropped the phone.

"You're not going to believe this!" I shouted, running back to the table. "There really is a treasure! No joke! Daddy read about it in Uncle Benjie's papers, and he says we're all going to search like crazy for the secret panel when we get back to North Haven."

"But we're here *now*," said Alice.

"Of course, dummy!" I said. "That's what's so exciting. We'll find it before Mummy and Daddy get back, and they'll be so grateful, they'll forget to get mad at us for staying here in the first place."

Alice and Minnow both brightened up at the idea. "But what is the treasure, Allegra?" Alice asked.

"Daddy's keeping that a secret," I told her, "but judging by how happy he sounded, it's got to be at least as good as diamonds."

We decided to go to bed early and get a good night's rest so that we could start hunting first thing in the morning, but about six hours later, I woke up with a jump.

It was absolutely quiet, but I knew I had heard some strange kind of sound. I waited, and after a minute or so, I heard it again: a loud clattering followed by a groan. I don't get scared easily, but this time I was terrified.

"Alice!" I whispered. "Wake up!"

Alice and I share a room in North Haven, and Minnow sleeps in a tiny room next to my parents. I've often wished I had a room of my own, but that night, I was glad of company.

"Alice!" I hissed. I leaned over and thumped her on the shoulder.

"What's wrong?" Alice mumbled. "I want to sleep!"

Then she heard the noise, too, and sat bolt upright. "You can come to my bed if you're afraid," she said.

"That's a big help!" I said. "What about Minnow? She's alone, remember, and she's only seven."

Suddenly, the clatter turned into a noise like giant hailstones on a tin roof, except it came from inside the house. The moaning mounted to a howl. I realized that whatever the other noise was, the howl belonged to Minnow.

"We'd better see what she's up to," I told Alice. "You come, too. Safety in numbers!"

After turning on the bedside lamp, I peeked into the hall. Everything looked normal. The two of us made a dash for Minnow's room, flipped on the light, and slammed the door behind us.

Minnow was hiding under the covers. When she heard the door slam, she moaned again.

"It's all right," said Alice. "It's only us."

Minnow poked her head out. Her hair was damp and all messed up, and her face was streaked with tears. Alice sat down on the bed and put her arms around her.

"Ouch!" cried Minnow. "Stop that!"

"What's the matter?" I asked. "What was that noise?"

"Murdering thieves after the treasure!" Minnow sobbed.

"Nonsense!" I said. "If it were murderers, we'd be dead by now, and thieves wouldn't be so noisy."

I wasn't really convinced myself, but it did the job with Minnow. She sniffed and wiped her tears.

"Whoever it was is gone now, anyway," I said.

We sat quietly and listened for a moment. All we could

hear were insects batting softly against the window screen, like rain.

"We ought to turn the light off, or the bugs will get in where the screen is torn," I said. "Do you think you can get to sleep now, Minnow?"

"No," said Minnow. "My skin hurts too much."

"What do you mean?" asked Alice. "Show me!"

Minnow raised her nightgown. The part of her that was usually covered by her bathing suit was bright red. The rest was just light brown. I felt a little guilty; we ought to have known she couldn't take so much sun.

"That must hurt like crazy!" I said. "Wait here, and I'll get the ointment."

It took all my courage to dash to the bathroom and grab the first-aid kit. Even Alice didn't offer to come along. But nothing jumped out at me, and I got back to Minnow's room safe and sound. I rubbed the ointment on her skin and gave her some baby aspirin, the way I saw my mother do once the summer before. Then I said that we should take a look downstairs.

Alice shuddered. "Downstairs? Are you crazy? Let's stay here and lock the door."

"Coward!" I said. "I'm going to turn on all the lights and make sure everything is safe. But you don't have to come if you don't want to."

I held my breath, hoping Alice would come, too

"Oh, all right!" she groaned. "You stay here, Minnow. We'll be right back."

"Stay here alone? I'd rather die!" said Minnow. She scrambled out of bed, wincing from her sunburn.

We didn't have to go far to see what had happened. Minnow had left her shopping bag at the top of the stairs. Some kind of animal had gnawed through the paper, and the shells had all gone cascading down the steps.

Minnow was so mad that she forgot to be scared. She ran down and started picking up the shells.

"I wonder what kind of animal likes glue?" I said. "Whatever it is, it must be your first cousin, Minnow!"

An animal wasn't as frightening as murdering thieves, so we were a little braver about looking around. When we turned on the kitchen light, a squirrel started flying around the room, knocking over pots and cups and glasses as it leapt from wall to wall.

Minnow giggled, and Alice hooted with relief. We opened the door and chased it out. Then we looked at the kitchen clock. It was three-thirty.

"What a weird time to be awake!" said Alice. "Do you think we should have breakfast?"

"What, for instance?" I asked. "Mussel broth with gin?"

I picked up the empty gin bottle and dropped it into the trash can. "Daddy is going to be furious if he can't have his gin and tonic when he comes back," I told Alice.

"He can have vodka and tonic instead," said Alice. "There's still plenty of vodka."

I went to the liquor cabinet and looked in. Alice was right. There were two full bottles of vodka, a lot of tonic water – and a can of peanuts! None of us had dreamed of looking in the liquor cabinet when we were making our search for supplies, and of course Alice is too absentminded to notice a thing like peanuts when her bird brain is concentrating on "eye of newt, and toe of frog."

"Peanuts!" I screamed.

"For breakfast?" asked Minnow, looking shocked.

"For a midnight snack," I said.

41

We sat around the kitchen table and popped peanuts into our mouths until there wasn't even a grain of salt left in the can. After mussels with gin, they were reassuring.

"You'll feel better tomorrow, Minnow," I promised as we tramped back upstairs to bed. "We'll hunt for the treasure all day if you like, and we'll eat like kings. I've planned a whole menu out of Daddy's book, and believe me, it's going to be a feast!"

CHAPTER FOUR

I thought I would sleep late the next morning, but instead, I exploded into wide-awakeness at exactly five-thirty. It was a clear day; I could almost count the tiny buildings spotted along the mainland coast. The Camden hills rose up behind them, blue and lumpy against the sky. They looked like Minnow, humped up under her blue blanket the night before.

A little shiver of guilt ran through me as I remembered my sister's sunburn. Poor Minnow! Had she been able to get any sleep at all? I tiptoed into her room to check and was relieved to see the familiar mound under the covers. She had obviously slept like a log all night long, in the same position.

Minnow is a scream, I thought fondly. She always sleeps crouched up, with her bottom higher than her head, burrowed under the bedclothes as if she were hibernating. But you'd think she would suffocate! I reached out and gently tugged at the blanket, just enough to uncover her nose.

Instead of Minnow's nose – instead of *any* part of Minnow – I found three stuffed bears, the legless doll, and a damp sneaker. And at that exact moment, there was a loud crash and a splintering noise so close behind me that I screamed and jumped about a foot in the air.

"Oh, phooey!" said Minnow.

She was on her hands and knees in the corner of the room that you can't see when you open her door, holding a screwdriver and surrounded by slivers of wood and plaster.

My stomach felt weak, and I suddenly noticed how cold I was in my bare feet and my nightgown. "Just what do you think you're doing?"

"I found the panel," Minnow told me matter-of-factly. "Only it's the wrong panel. All this one has are water pipes."

I groaned. "For heaven's sake, Minnow! Every room in this house has a panel like that. If that's where the treasure was, Daddy would have found it years ago. He opens it every time he has to fix the plumbing."

Minnow reached her arm into the hole up to her shoulder and explored the dark space – something I would never dare to do because of mice and spiders. She groped around a little and finally pulled out a china horse with one leg missing. When I saw it, for a split second I felt all clutched up and scared. Then I remembered why: That was Alice's horse. When I was even younger than Minnow, I broke it one morning, and was so frightened of what Alice would say that I hid it and let Alice think it was lost.

"Well, what do you know!" I said calmly, and before Minnow could ask any questions, I grabbed it and slipped out of the room.

Still in my nightgown, I ran downstairs and across the cold, dewy grass to the raspberry patch. Then I flung the horse into the dead center of the patch, where the brambles are the thickest and thorniest. My conscience was troubling me just the tiniest bit, but I ignored it and concentrated on looking for wild raspberries. It had been a late spring, and the berries were barely beginning to ripen, but I hoped to get enough for breakfast. If only we had cream to pour on top!

"Oh, if only we could make cocoa for breakfast!" I said aloud. "If only we had eggs and bacon!"

I make a point of thinking out loud from time to time, to cure myself of the embarrassed feeling it gives me. Why should I embarrass myself, all alone in nature? It just shows how inhibited I am. Whereas Minnow runs around stark naked, and Alice shouts poetry at ducks. I'd rather be like that, but I'm a little old for nudity, and I don't know many poems. Only one psalm and some Longfellow that my father quotes so often that I couldn't forget it if I tried.

I edged my way gingerly around the raspberry patch, keeping an eye out for hornets' nests. Hornets' nests are beautiful, puffy, papery balls that you long to touch until you see what's coming out of them. Then you run. But it's hard to run in brambles, especially if you're in bare feet and your nightgown, so I was careful.

Most of the berries were still hard and pale, but I picked a few ripe ones here and there, flicking off the little green bugs that like them, too. The smell of wild raspberries under a hot sun was almost enough for breakfast by itself. I breathed in and out deeply a few times before treating the raspberry patch to a dramatic rendition of "The Children's Hour."

"The Children's Hour" happens to be one of my least favorite poems in the English language; it's too sentimental for my taste. But I went through it with feeling that morning to loosen up my inhibitions:

45

"From my study I see in the lamplight,
Descending the broad hall stair,
Grave Alice, and laughing Allegra,
And Edith with golden hair."

My voice sounded too silly to believe. I blushed in spite of myself, alone in the raspberry patch.

All around me, the white-throated sparrows were piping, *Poor Sam Peabody-Peabody-Peabody*: two long, high notes and nine quick, low ones, over and over. Some crows were kicking up a racket in the fir trees, and way up in the sky, an osprey circled with anxious, faraway cries. I decided I liked bird noises better than my own, so I shut up.

When I went back indoors with my berries, I found Minnow already busy with her shells and glue. She had covered every coffee can in the house. Now she was working on the percolator.

I wasn't sure how my mother would like that. I wasn't sure you could *use* a percolator that was covered with shells and school glue, but I let Minnow do it anyway. After all, we were making tea, not coffee in the mornings. My mother could deal with the problem when she got back. No matter how critical you are if you're a sister, once you start being a parent, too, you tend to get lenient. Otherwise, you'd go crazy.

It wasn't the percolator that shocked me when I saw Minnow. It was her clothes. She was wearing clean white socks and school shoes, a skirt, and a lacy blouse, and her hair was tied back with a pink ribbon. For a minute, I thought the emotion of the night before had driven her out of her mind. First a whole day of nudity and now this!

"Minnow!" I exclaimed. "What on earth are you all dressed up for?"

Minnow looked up innocently. "Church," she said.

"Church?" I repeated. "Poor Minnow! It must be sunstroke!"
Ordinarily we *do* go to church in North Haven. My mother
says it's the only place she really feels religion because it's so
small and simple, with salt air leaking through the windows
and lots of hymn-singing. But we slip in and slip out, pretending we don't recognize any of the other people. Otherwise, you
get trapped and asked to a luncheon party. Or some creep
comes up and tells you that his great-aunt knew your grand-
mother's college roommate.

"Church is out of the question," I told Minnow. "It's seven
miles back to the village. Besides, we don't want anyone to
know we're here."

Minnow's face fell. Not that she's fond of sermons, but she
gets a big kick out of singing the doxology. She likes the part
where you yell, "Praise ye all creatures here below!" Minnow
yells, that is, and the old ladies turn around and frown.

What's more, I happen to know that when all the other children put a quarter on the plate, Minnow takes one off. Alice
and I keep telling her it's not just sinful, it's illegal. But she
swears she'll pay it back with interest when she grows up.

"Be reasonable, Minnow," I said. "Even if we started walking
now, we wouldn't get there on time. And think how tired we
were the other day!"

"We don't have to carry our suitcases," said Minnow. But
she gave in.

Just then, Alice wandered into the kitchen, looking the opposite of Minnow. Her blond hair was frizzed up around her
head so wildly that I suspected it would take an hour to brush
the knots out. She was wearing a sweatshirt over her nightgown, and although she had on socks, they didn't match.

She gave me a blue-eyed stare and whispered, "*'Tis almost
morning; I would have thee gone.*"

47

"It's been morning for hours," I told her crossly, "and anyway, we got here first."

"Oh, good morning, Legs!" said Alice pleasantly, as if she hadn't really noticed me before.

"Same to you," I said. "Did you and Romeo get any sleep?"

Alice rarely answers back. It's absolutely no fun teasing her. Besides, she had just caught sight of the raspberries.

"Oh, Legs, you angel!" she cried, and she threw herself on the berries like someone who was dying of hunger.

"Alice," Minnow said with a reproachful glance at me, "Allegra says we can't go to church."

Alice munched thoughtfully. "Legs is right," she said. "It wouldn't do. Let's have church here!"

Minnow looked scandalized. "Here in our house?"

"Out on the point," said Alice. "We'll make a cross."

The point Alice meant is the highest spot on our property. It juts out over the water like the prow of a boat, and it's a better place than most to have a church. We tied two sticks together to make the cross and stood in a row, singing the doxology at the top of our lungs. Then we sang "Onward, Christian Soldiers." The hymn seemed to make more sense there than it did in our church in the village.

"We each ought to say a prayer," said Alice.

Alice isn't usually that keen on religion, so I knew she had something up her sleeve.

"What for?" I asked.

"It might be unlucky not to," said Alice. "You go first."

I recited the 121st psalm, which is the only one I know. It starts, "I will lift up mine eyes unto the hills, from whence cometh my help." I used to think that meant the Camden hills, across Penobscot Bay, so it was appropriate.

"*The sun shall not strike thee by day nor the moon by night,*" I continued while my mind flashed back to Minnow's sunburn and the squirrel on the stairs.

"Please, God, don't let anything worse happen!" I added when I got to the end. "Amen. Your turn, Alice."

Alice clasped her hands, gazed dreamily at the horizon, and started wailing in a voice that probably carried all the way to the mainland:

"*Come, civil night,*
Thou sober-suited matron, all in black,
And learn me how to lose a winning match,
Played for a pair of stainless maidenhoods."

I made a lunge for her and knocked her to the ground. It was only soft pine needles, so neither of us got hurt, but at least Alice shut up.

"I might have known!" I said. "I might have *known* you just wanted another chance to show off! Prayer, my eye! Why, that's practically X-rated!"

"Besides," Minnow added primly, "'learn me' is bad grammar."

Minnow's voice was accompanied by a little hissing sound. I spun around and caught her squatting a few feet away with her underpants down. "I needed to pee," she announced, as if it weren't obvious.

"Minnow!" I gasped. "In the house of the Lord? Are you out of your mind? This is hallowed earth!"

Alice started plucking pine needles out of her socks. "You know something, Allegra? You're hopelessly conventional."

"Well, I think you're both disgusting!" I said, and I marched self-righteously through the fir trees toward the house. Who else but me would get sisters like that?

When I reached home, I sat down with my father's book on wild foods to review the day's menu. There was a chance that if I made it sound appetizing enough, I could persuade Alice and Minnow to help me.

"What we need first is bayberry leaves," I told them as they came through the door. "If you steam them with seafood, it tastes better, and you can make tea out of them, too."

"What's a bayberry?" asked Alice.

"I'm not sure," I said, "but I think there are some on the path to the beach."

"That's deadly nightshade," said Minnow. "I heard Daddy warning Mummy."

Alice shuddered. "Let's skip that course. What else is on the menu?"

I turned the page. "How about common cattail? This book says you can eat pretty much the whole thing. First, you use the bloom spines for a cooked vegetable – "

"What are bloom spines?" asked Minnow.

"Don't interrupt," I said. "Where was I? Oh, yes, you can also use the pollen for pancake flour, and if you peel the stalk, it's not unlike cucumber."

"I hate cucumber," said Alice.

"It doesn't actually say it's *like* cucumber," I reasoned. "Besides, we have to eat something today. It says in the preface that we can feast our way to survival."

Alice and Minnow agreed to give cattails a try. "But what else?" asked Minnow.

"Look at the picture!" I told her. "That little boy is enjoying a bowlful of stir-fried Irish moss!"

"Yuck!" said Minnow. "He sounds like a creep."

Alice said she was willing to try, as long as we didn't add any bayberry leaves.

"But that's not all," I said. "We're going to have sea-urchin roe and Cancer irroratus."

"Cancer what?" asked Alice.

"Irroratus," I repeated. "That's rock crabs. They hang around the seaweed at low tide. The tide's pretty low now – let's go look!"

"No," said Minnow firmly. "Let's look for treasure."

I opened my mouth to remind her that you couldn't eat diamonds, besides the fact that it was another beautiful day, but I didn't have the heart to preach at her. Now that I knew there really was a treasure, hunting stopped being a rainy-day activity and became more exciting. After all, the crabs could wait, and there would be lots more sunny weather.

We decided to start in the living room. Most of the secret panels in stories are found behind old family portraits, or above a medieval fireplace, as I remember. So Alice and Minnow and I systematically thumped and tapped our way around. It was kind of pointless because except for the one that led to the plumbing, there weren't any panels at all in the living room, secret or otherwise. It was just plain wall, streaked with mildew and fingerprints, to say nothing of the place where Alice had thrown a baby bottle full of grape juice when she was ten months old.

"Let's save the rest of the house for later," I said. "The tide will be coming in by now."

Nobody objected, so I sent Minnow off to change into a bathing suit, and tried to remember where my father kept the fishing nets.

We found our first crab in a little pool left by the tide.

"Got him!" I shouted as I scooped it up with my net. "He isn't very big, though. Do you think they puff up when you boil them, like hot dogs?"

51

"Oh, are you supposed to boil them?" asked Alice. "Good! I was afraid we had to crunch them up raw and let the blood run down our chins."

I nearly threw up. "Cut it out, Alice! Just shut up and help me look for them. Now, watch how I do it."

I wasn't very successful. Actually, it was Minnow who found the most. Alice wasn't any help at all because she was being Juliet again. She lifted the heavy mops of seaweed the way I showed her, but she didn't look underneath. The biggest crab of the day was right under her nose, and she didn't even notice. It scuttered off before I could get there with my net.

"Alice!" I yelled at her. "Don't you *care?*"

She looked at me with her sweet smile and quoted:
"Is there no pity sitting in the clouds
That sees into the bottom of my grief?
O sweet my mother, cast me not away!"

"Then cast yourself away!" I told her. "Go to the other end of the beach, and take Romeo with you!"

Alice wandered off, trailing her net after her. I sighed as I heard it snagging on the barnacles, and made a mental note to sew it up again before my father came home.

Minnow and I caught eleven crabs in all. They were kind of small, and I doubted they would fill us up for supper, but the tide was getting too high to hunt for more.

We could still hear Alice. She was standing on a tall, seaweed covered rock at the far end of the beach, chanting:
"O! bid me leap, rather than marry Paris,
From off the battlements of yonder tower;
Or walk – "
Suddenly, she let out a loud shriek and disappeared.

"Okay, okay!" I shouted. "You don't have to marry Paris!"

There was total silence. Minnow and I ran to where we last saw Alice and found her sitting in a nest of wet seaweed. Tears were rolling down her cheeks.

Minnow gasped. "What happened?"

"I fell," said Alice. "I think I broke my leg."

"How about Romeo?" I asked. "Is he still in one piece?"

As soon as the words were out, I wished I hadn't tried to be funny, because it was obvious that Alice was really in pain. It wasn't the moment to tease her.

I crouched down and inspected the leg. "Can you stand on it?"

Alice leaned on my shoulder as she pulled herself up. "I think I can walk back to the house if you help me."

Minnow and I both helped her. She managed to limp up the path and through the kitchen door before collapsing

All at once, I panicked and felt like a younger sister again, instead of the eleven-year-old mastermind. "What should I do?" I asked her. "Should I call Dr. Pierce?"

"That would ruin everything!" said Alice. "Let's have lunch, and then I'll take a nap. I'm sure it will get better. It can't be broken if I could get all the way home on it."

There wasn't much lunch, but Minnow and I did our best. We boiled some of the periwinkles, and picked a teacup of raspberries for Alice. As for the crabs, it was their lucky day. The tide had carried them out to sea, along with our fishing nets.

After lunch, Minnow and I looked at the remaining periwinkles and decided that if they were supper, we wouldn't make it through the night. We propped up Alice with sofa cushions in the living room and gave her a couple of my Nancy Drews to read. Then we went out to the woods to look for chanterelles.

Chanterelles are not the only edible mushrooms in our woods, but Minnow and I hadn't the slightest idea what the others looked like, so we left them alone. We were afraid of picking an amanita by mistake. A single amanita can kill a whole family. Every time Minnow saw one, she let out a scream, although I told her they wouldn't jump out and bite her.

"You can even pick it up, Minnow," I told her. "See? Just wipe your hand after you've touched it."

I threw the amanita into a briar patch and wiped my hand on my jeans. Reassuring Minnow is one thing, and dying of mushroom poisoning is another.

We gathered a whole bagful of chanterelles. We could have found a lot more if we had gone deeper into the woods, but I was afraid of getting lost.

"Let's go back," I said. "We have more than we need for supper. I want to see how Alice is."

It was no easy job getting Minnow to come back. She had found a raspberry patch in a sunny clearing, and a lot of the berries were ripe.

"Just one more!" she kept begging.

I ate a few myself. All the berries we picked at lunch had been for Alice, because of her ankle.

"Come on, Minnow," I said finally. "Enough is enough."

"I'm coming," she promised, pushing her way farther into the patch.

"I'm leaving!" I warned. "I hope you know your way home."

Even that didn't get her. All I could see was the top of her brown ponytail over the green leaves. "Just that big juicy one over there," she called. "Then I'll come."

All of a sudden, there was a big scream, and Minnow came. When I said you couldn't run in a raspberry patch, I was wrong. Minnow proved it. She came tearing out of those brambles, screaming her head off and followed by a swarm of yellow jackets.

"Turn left at the crossing!" I shouted after her, but I didn't need to. Minnow knew her way home.

When I got back, both sisters were lying on the living room sofa. Minnow's face was tear-streaked, and she had the hiccups. Alice didn't look much better.

"Two down and one to go!" I said. "It looks as if I'm running a hospital. How many stings, Minnow?"

There was one on her neck and three on the back of her right hand. She got off easy.

"You can *die* of bee stings," Minnow sobbed. "Maybe they were killer bees."

"They were yellow jackets," I told her. "Did you put baking soda on her, Alice?"

Alice looked pityingly at Minnow and recited:

"What devil art thou that dost torment me thus?
This torture should be roar'd in dismal hell – "

"Maybe," I said, "but first you could try baking soda."

"I can't get up," said Alice.

I made a paste with soda and water. Personally, I never thought it helped all that much, but Minnow was still young enough so that any treatment cheered her up. I smeared her bites with the paste and put bandages on top for good measure. Then I turned to Alice.

"How's your ankle? Let's see it."

Alice stuck her leg out stiffly. "It's swollen, but it only hurts when I try to walk on it."

It certainly was swollen, all red and puffy.

"Some people are like that naturally!" said Alice. "Can you imagine a whole lifetime with thick ankles?"

She stuck out the other foot for comparison. Alice really does have pretty feet, and if she was feeling well enough to admire them, there couldn't be much wrong with her.

"I can't remember what you do for sprained ankles," I said. "Do you soak them in hot water or cold water?"

"Let's try one foot in each," Minnow suggested.

"Hot," said Alice firmly. "With Mummy's bath salts."

Alice hates cold water. She only swims in Maine out of principle. I knew she wouldn't put her foot in a cold tub even if I showed her in print that it was the right thing to do, so I ran her a hot bath. She spent two hours in it, finishing a Nancy Drew.

Nobody had much appetite that night. I served the rest of the periwinkles cold with dressing, and the mushrooms hot with plenty of salt and pepper. It was a good meal, considering, but we pushed the food around our plates.

"Come on, eat up!" I urged the others as I toyed with a forkful of chanterelles. "We should be counting our blessings. At least we're not at Aunt Ruth's house."

"I'd give anything for some bread and milk right now," said Alice.

"Aunt Ruth is always saying, *Eat to live, don't live to eat*," I reminded her. "This is an adventure in survival, remember? It's exciting!"

My sisters didn't look very excited. Minnow pushed her plate away, and Alice limped off to the sofa for the night. I had our room to myself, but I didn't enjoy it as much as I thought I would. I lay there listening to the foghorns out in the bay and the worry of moths against the screen.

Four more days! I thought. My heart sank at the prospect of keeping Alice and Minnow fed, cheerful, and free from accidents for another four days.

Then I scolded myself for being such a coward. Here we were, alone in Maine with the whole place to ourselves, and somewhere in the house was a hidden treasure! I'd concentrate on the search for the next few days and stop fussing about commonplace things. After all, nothing terrible could happen to us, could it? Even if we didn't eat at all until Thursday, we wouldn't starve to death.

"An adventure in survival!" I whispered into the dark. "We're surviving so far – and I'd rather be here than any place else in the world!"

CHAPTER FIVE

Cold mushrooms hardly make the world's most appealing breakfast, but it was drizzling on Monday morning, and it hardly seemed worthwhile to go out through the fog in search of berries. They say that hunger is the best appetizer. Now I know what that means. We shoveled in those chanterelles as if they were waffles with maple syrup.

Alice sat with both feet immersed in the mussel pot, which I had filled with hot water. Her ankle was still swollen, and she was grouchy because I woke her up coming through the living room. She had read my Nancy Drews until two o'clock in the morning. Alice's idea of heaven is a place where you can read until you fall asleep, and then sleep as late as you want. I like early morning best, especially in Maine, so I make her turn the light off, but that night she had been alone.

"How many more days do we have to eat this garbage?" asked Alice.

I noticed that she emptied her plate before complaining – talk of ingratitude! I was about to say four until I looked at her face and at Minnow's. They were a little woebegone. I was responsible for the worry week, adventure in survival or not, so it was my job to keep their spirits up.

"Two full days," I said, forcing myself to sound cheerful. "Plus the beginning of the day Mummy and Daddy come home, and the rest of today."

"The rest of today?" Alice glanced at the kitchen clock and back at me. It was only ten to eight, but she didn't comment on it. Even when she's grouchy, Alice is nice.

"I don't think I can go outside this morning," she said, changing the subject. "What are you and Minnow planning in the way of food?"

"Not mussels," Minnow said decidedly. "I'm never going to eat anything that has been cooked in that pot again. Yuck!"

Alice splashed a little water toward Minnow. "My feet are cleaner than your hands. If you handed me a slice of carrot cake with cream cheese frosting right this instant, I wouldn't accept it."

Minnow's eyes narrowed. I intervened before she could answer back. "I'm afraid it's going to be mushrooms again. We know they're good, so we'd better have them to fall back on. Then I thought I'd get some periwinkles."

"I'm tired of periwinkles," said Alice. "Didn't you say something about sea-urchin roe? That might taste like caviar!"

"It might," I agreed, "but the book says you have to crack them open while they're still alive, and eat them raw with a spoon. How about summer greens? We haven't eaten anything green for days."

"We probably already have scurvy," said Alice gloomily. "It makes your hair and teeth fall out, and then you die."

Minnow looked up from the percolator. She had been pasting shells in patterns on the lid. "Are you joking, Alice?" she asked, in a voice that showed she was afraid the answer would be no.

Alice groaned. "Of course I'm joking! Have you planned anything for dessert, Legs?"

"Carrot cake with cream cheese frosting," I said.

Alice looked crosser than ever. She stood up, winced in an exaggerated way, and limped toward the living room sofa, leaving a trail of wet footprints behind her.

"I'm sorry," I said. "I know that wasn't funny. But listen. Some of these recipes don't sound too bad!"

I followed her into the living room, skimming through the pages of my father's book. "You can make fantastic salads out of all this green stuff that grows along the shore: chickweed and beach parsley and wild mint. And how about steamed lambs' quarters? All you do is – "

Alice interrupted me. "Lambs' quarters? Gross! Front or hind?"

"It's a plant, stupid!" I told her. "Daddy calls it orach, and it says here it's a botanical relative of spinach. Oh, and here's another recipe for sea urchins – roasted, not raw!"

Minnow made a sick noise from the kitchen, and I began to panic. "Well, you can make a delicious, crunchy snack out of dried seaweed," I said. "Or you can make stew out of it if you add onions and beach peas and herbs. That sounds good, doesn't it?"

"No," said Alice.

I sighed and shut the book. "Well, it's going to be periwinkles and mushrooms then, and we'd better go mushrooming first, because the tide won't be low until ten. I don't suppose you could have a look for the treasure while we're gone?"

Alice pointed at her feet, which were unnaturally pale and clean and all wrinkled from so much soaking. "I can hardly move, Allegra! I swear, every time I wiggle my ankle, I'm in mortal agony."

I brought the pile of *National Geographics* over to the sofa for her, in case she ran out of Nancy Drews. "We're leaving now," I said. "Will you be okay?"

Alice leaned back and flung her hand dramatically to her brow.

"Farewell! God knows when we shall meet again.
I have a faint cold fear thrills through my veins,
That almost freezes up the heat of life."

She looked awfully comfortable for someone in mortal agony, and I began to wonder if she would make as much fuss about her ankle if it weren't drizzling outside. You could hardly blame her.

Minnow and I put on slickers and started down the road. The drizzle had thickened into a light rain, and the grass was so wet that our sneakers got sopped through right away. The cuffs of my jeans felt clammy around my ankles, and they were flecked with grass seed.

You couldn't see more than a few yards ahead because of the fog, and no birds were singing. Instead, we heard two fog-horns mooing gloomily out in the bay, one medium low and one very low, like a cow calling her calf.

Ordinarily, I rather like that sort of weather. I'd settle for one rainy day a week on North Haven, just so that I could stay indoors and read a book or two. But we weren't reading. We were mushrooming.

Minnow's feet squished inside her sneakers, but she didn't seem to mind. In fact, she was singing. She started with the doxology and moved on to "Ninety-nine Bottles of Beer on the Wall," which is hardly one of my favorites, unless I'm on a school bus trying to enrage the driver. But at least it was keeping Minnow cheerful.

Once we were in the woods, the rain wasn't so bad, but it was unbearably humid under the dripping branches, and the smell of wet pine bark was so strong that it hurt the back of my nose. We had to go way in before we found any chanterelles because we had picked all the close ones the day before. I moved from mossy patch to mossy patch, keeping an eye out for those little dabs of orange. Minnow stuck right behind me.

"What's the use of following me like that?" I asked. "I've picked all the ones around here. Look somewhere else!"

"I'm going where you go," said Minnow. "That way, if there's a hornets' nest, you'll step on it first."

"Gee, thanks!" I said.

I let her follow me for a while, but by the time she had sung down to sixty-three bottles of beer on the wall, she began to get on my nerves.

"Minnow, you either stop that or find your own mushroom patch," I told her. "I can't stand it anymore!"

"I can't stop until I get to *one*," said Minnow. She wandered reluctantly off, still singing.

The mushrooms were few and far between, and I was beginning to feel discouraged until I came to a mossy mound that was positively covered with chanterelles. Flopping down on my knees, I picked with both hands. In no time at all, my bag was full.

"Minnow!" I called. "I've got enough. Let's go home!"

Minnow didn't answer. All I could hear was water dropping from the branches.

"Minnow!" I screamed.

Not a word from her. Not even singing, and I was sure she

hadn't had time to get down to "no more bottles of beer on the wall." Even if she had, knowing Minnow, she would start putting them back on and work up to a hundred again – a sure way to drive bus drivers crazy, to say nothing of your own sister.

Beer bottles or not, I didn't want to lose Minnow. I began to run through the trees, shouting at the top of my lungs. Pretty soon, I heard Minnow shouting back, and I found her, not nearly as far away as I was afraid she would be. Some days, your voice just doesn't carry.

"Why did you wander off like that?" I demanded.

"You told me to," said Minnow.

"Well, don't do it again," I said. "We've got plenty of mushrooms. Let's go home."

"Good!" said Minnow. "Which way is home?"

Looking around, I realized that I hadn't the vaguest idea. I hadn't kept track of where I was going while I chased after Minnow. Now we were both lost.

"Don't be scared!" I told Minnow. "Let's think."

"Who's scared?" asked Minnow. She grabbed my hand.

I thought hard, trying to remember things people do in books when they get lost. They see where the sun is, for one thing, but the sun wasn't out that day. There's also some business about which side of trees the moss grows on, but in North Haven, the moss grows on all sides. Or you follow a stream to the shore, but there was no stream nearby. Then, very faintly, I heard the foghorns.

"I know!" I said. "All we have to do is follow that sound. It will lead us to the water, and we can walk home along the shore."

Following the sound of a foghorn is not like walking toward someone who is calling you. It's a much more spread-out noise. But we pushed our way through the trees – a feat in itself in North Haven, where lots of the pines are dead and

63

spiky. I got a big scratch on my cheek, and Minnow nearly poked her eye out. Huge black ravens kept flapping out of the thickets, screaming bloody murder. We were dead tired when, unexpectedly, we stepped out onto a road.

"Oh, no!" I groaned. "We must have been going in the wrong direction. There's not supposed to be a road between the woods and the beach!"

"Who cares?" said Minnow. "This is better. No more scratchy branches! We can just follow the road home."

"Yes, but which way is home?" I asked.

We looked both ways. Inland roads on North Haven are pretty much the same, and I saw nothing to help me recognize this one. It could be any road at all, and I had heard that there are twenty miles of them on the island. I wasn't about to walk twenty miles.

"Let's think some more," I told Minnow. "We need a rest, anyway."

We sat down by the side of the road and thought. I took off my slicker, and Minnow rolled up the legs of her jeans. The rain had stopped, the fog was lifting fast, and we felt as if we were in the middle of a steam bath.

"It's funny," I said. "We really did follow that horn. It sounds much closer now, you have to admit."

"You can't see any lighthouse from our windows," Minnow pointed out. "Maybe those foghorns were in the wrong direction."

Why hadn't I thought of that myself? What a dumb mistake! Just because I heard foghorns from my bed at night didn't mean they were in our part of the bay. For all I knew, they were on the other side of the island.

"Why didn't you say so before?" I demanded crossly.

"You never asked," said Minnow.

Fighting about it wasn't going to help, so I shut my eyes and tried to depend on instinct, but I wasn't very optimistic. My instincts didn't seem to be helping me much lately.

"I give up," I told Minnow finally. "How can I tell which way is home if I don't even know what road this is?"

"Sure you do, Allegra," said Minnow. "This is the road to Crabtree Point."

"Why on earth didn't you say so?" I shouted.

"You never asked which road it was," said Minnow. "You just asked which way was home."

After I knew it was the road to Crabtree Point, everything came back to me. We turned left and then left again, and before long, we were at our mailbox. It was empty except for an ad from a supermarket in Rockland.

"Peanut butter!" I read, my mouth watering. "Jelly doughnuts!" I didn't bother with prices. I would have paid ten times the normal price for a jelly doughnut.

"I'd settle for a nickel's worth of penny candy at Waterman's," said Minnow wistfully. "Couldn't we go to Waterman's, Allegra?"

"We've done enough walking, and we haven't got a nickel with us," I told her. "Besides, I'm afraid we're going to be late for low tide."

We were. All the rocks were covered by the time we reached the beach, and the water had begun to creep up the shore.

"Goody!" cried Minnow. "No more survival!"

I looked at her scornfully. "I'm glad *someone's* happy. But just what are we going to eat? I didn't notice a lot of enthusiasm for those mushrooms at breakfast, and more mushrooms is all we've got."

Minnow and I decided to cool off with a swim. It's funny how when the fog lifts, the heat seems hotter than the normal kind.

Swimming at almost-low tide is creepy because you bump your knees on all sorts of dark things underwater. I'm a coward about them, even though I keep telling myself they're only rocks and seaweed that were uncovered a while before. So we just dunked, in the nude, since Alice wasn't there to turn up her nose at us. Minnow was right. It did feel warmer without a bathing suit.

On our way back to the house, we collected a whole heap of things my father's book said were edible: orach, cattails, rosehips, and kelp. It was exciting. I had always known those things were there, but had never thought of them as food.

Orach is a spade-shaped leaf that grows in straggly clumps at the top of the beach. Kelp is seaweed: a rubbery rope with a wide, flat piece at the end. When we were younger, we used to attach kelp ropes to the seat of our jeans and call them lion tails. In fact, Minnow still does.

Cattails are swamp reeds with brown things like fuzzy hot dogs at the top, and rose hips are little red tomato-like balls that grow on the wild briar rose.

"But these aren't red," said Minnow. "They're green."

"They're rose hips all the same," I assured her. "Maybe they turn red when you cook them, like lobsters. Only the recipe doesn't say anything about cooking them."

"They're hard as rocks," said Minnow, pinching one. "I bet you have to cook them all day, like stew meat. They'll never be done in time for lunch."

"Then we'll have them for supper," I said. "Come on, let's get moving. Alice is probably bored to tears."

We found Alice on the sofa, in exactly the same position as when we left her. The only difference was that her feet were filthy, and there was a cobweb over her left ear.

"What have you been up to?" I asked.

"Up?" Alice repeated innocently. "I can't move! It was all I could do to get to the bathroom and back. I'll have lunch in here, please."

I was too hungry to ask questions, so I dropped the orach in boiling water, sauteed the mushrooms, and carried everything out to the living room on a tray.

Alice took one look and sighed. "Is that all? You can't be serious! Didn't you find any raspberries?"

"We got lost," I said. "If you're sick of mushrooms, try some orach. It's supposed to be very nutritious."

The orach looked and smelled like spinach – a welcome change from our usual menu that week – but my sisters eyed it suspiciously.

"That isn't deadly nightshade, is it, Legs?" asked Alice. She took a tiny mouthful, then spat it out.

"What's wrong now?" I asked.

I nibbled cautiously. It wasn't all that bad. Not nearly as good as it looked and smelled, but aside from the weird salty-sour taste and slimy texture, it got by. I mixed it with the mushrooms. They were even slimier, but I was hungry.

Alice finished a Nancy Drew while she ate, to keep her mind off her food. Reading during meals is strictly forbidden in our family, but I didn't say anything, not even when Minnow, inspired by Alice, reached for the *National Geographic* with the naked tribe. After all, I had promised them complete freedom. I would have read a book myself, but my mind was already on our next meal.

"We'll have some raw orach for supper," I told my sisters. "I'm making wild stew."

Alice gave me a blank stare and returned to her book.

"Stew is cooked," Minnow objected. "You said raw."

"Wild salad, then," I said. "The book says it's delicious."

I noticed that no one offered to help. Minnow, who usually trails after me like a puppy dog, went to check out her room for secret panels. As for Alice, she twisted around so that all I could see was her back and the soles of her feet.

I examined them more closely. "Where have you been, anyway? Your feet are absolutely disgusting!"

Alice turned a page.

"They never got that way just walking to the bathroom and back."

No answer.

"Come on," I said. "What have you been up to? I can't think of anywhere in the whole *house* that would turn your feet the color of Roquefort cheese."

Alice sighed. "If you *must* know, I was down in the cellar."

"The cellar?" I said. "And you couldn't even make it to the kitchen for lunch? Faker! What were you doing down there?"

Alice had suddenly become deaf, so I went to find out for myself.

No one ever uses our cellar because the floor is just packed earth and it's too damp and moldy to be good for storage. The last time I was down there was a year before, when I helped Minnow bury her pet turtle. Minnow didn't want to bury the thing outside in case some dog found it and dug it up, so we made a grave in the cellar.

I smiled, remembering how Minnow had wept and prayed, written a memorial poem, and then covered the place with a wedge of flagstone marked R.I.P. Then I laughed because I suddenly guessed what Alice had been doing. After feeling my way cautiously down the old steps that are apt to collapse in unexpected places, I ran over to the turtle's grave. Sure enough, there was a large hole and a pile of dirt with my mother's gardening trowel lying beside it. Alice has never been one to clean up after herself.

I took the trowel back up to the kitchen and left it in the sink for Alice to rinse off. After all, if she could get all the way to the cellar, she was well enough to start helping out a little. In fact, the more I thought about it, the madder I got. Why should I be chopping up stuff for supper while my sisters were hunting for treasure?

"Faker!" I muttered, picking up the paring knife.

"Is that you, Legs?" Alice shouted. "I'm sick of Nancy Drew. What else have you got?"

"*Mrs. Piggle-Wiggle*," I said, walking into the living room with the knife in one hand and a cattail bloom in the other.

Alice stared at me in horror. "You don't expect me to eat that thing for supper, do you?"

"Not this part, princess," I said. "The inside of the stalk. If that suits your highness."

"It doesn't," said Alice, "but I guess I have no choice."

"You can always go down to the cellar and dig for truffles," I told her. "Mummy's trowel is in the sink for you to clean at your convenience. Did you find anything interesting, by the way?"

Alice made a face and pulled a ragged piece of paper out of her pocket. "Only this."

I smoothed the paper and read aloud: "He came too early to his timely end, but while he lived he always had a friend."

Does that refer to Romeo, or to Tybalt?"

"Don't be idiotic!" said Alice. "Why didn't you tell me that Minnow planted that stinking turtle corpse down there?"

"You never asked," I said smugly, taking a lesson from Minnow herself. "I think that's pretty good poetry for a six-year-old. I remember, I told her she really meant '*un*timely end,' but Minnow said it didn't come out right that way. Did you find the turtle shell?"

Alice nodded. "I left it there. It was disgusting."

"If I were you, I wouldn't mention it to Minnow," I advised her. "She'd have a fit. Fill up the hole again, why don't you? Whatever gave you the idea of looking down there in the first place?"

"I remembered seeing the stone," said Alice. "How was I supposed to know it was only a grave?"

"Well, it sure wasn't a secret panel, in any case," I said. "Look on the ground floor from now on. It'll be easier on your foot."

"I'm not going to look at all," said Alice. "I bet the whole thing is some joke of Daddy's. You know why he wouldn't tell you what the treasure is? Because he doesn't know yet, that's why. He's going to buy us something in Boston the way he always does when he's off on a trip, and he's going to have us hunt for it."

"I don't know," I said slowly. "He didn't have that sort of voice when he told me. I think there really is something."

Alice shrugged. "Hunt for it yourself, then. What other books did you say you had?"

"Only *Mrs. Piggle-Wiggle*," I told her.

Alice groaned. "That's infantile! Why don't you read something challenging for a change?"

"Speak for yourself," I said. "You're the one who was too lazy to go to the library last week."

Alice looked desperate for a moment, but she soon brightened up again. "Minnow!" she bellowed. "Could you bring down *Caddie Woodlawn*? It's in my suitcase."

"You mean you never unpacked?" I asked Alice.

"What for?" she answered. "After lugging that bag all the way back from the boat, I wouldn't care if I never saw it again."

Minnow was a long time getting *Caddie Woodlawn*. Alice kept yelling instructions at her, but she couldn't find it.

"Under the socks, dummy!" Alice shouted.

"Okay, I'm looking!" Minnow shouted back.

"Look under the underpants, too. Hurry up!"

"I'm hurrying! Hold your horses!" Minnow yelled. But she still didn't come.

"Legs, can't *you* go?" asked Alice. "I know it's there."

"I'm busy," I said. "Get it yourself. You got down to the cellar and back, right?"

"That's why I have to rest now," Alice told me seriously. "I have to give the muscles time to grow back on the bone."

I didn't believe a word of it, but again, I had promised my sisters that we could do whatever we liked that week. If Alice liked to lie on a sofa with her feet up, it was all right with me as long as she didn't send me up and down stairs doing errands for her. I went back to the kitchen and started chopping kelp.

"It's about time!" said Alice when Minnow came down with the book. "Where did you find it?"

"Under the socks," said Minnow. She had a guilty look on her face. When I called her to come help chop, she slipped outside as if she hadn't heard me.

The wild salad was not a wild success. It may have been because we sat around reading all afternoon and didn't work up an appetite. I noticed that Minnow wasn't even licking the school glue on her fingers. She wiped them on her jeans instead.

In any case, there was something odd about that salad. First of all, the kelp was simply disgusting. I noticed later that the book said you should dry it out first, but I hadn't had time.

And I must have used the wrong part of the cattail hearts be-cause they were awfully stringy. As for the rosehips, they were so tart they made your tongue curl up. The raw orach was okay, though.

Alice only ate the orach leaves, but she was polite about the rest of the salad. "At least it *looks* beautiful!" she said. "It must have been a lot of trouble, Legs. We'd all be starving if it weren't for you."

"We're starving *now*," I said bitterly. "This stuff is edible, but it doesn't fill you up. Pass the mushrooms."

Minnow didn't touch a thing. She just sat there looking guilty and a little pale.

"Try the orach, Minnow," I pleaded. "Just one leaf? It's not so bad, I promise!"

"No, thanks," said Minnow.

"You can have my mushrooms if you like," said Alice.

"No, thanks," Minnow repeated. "I don't even want my own."

"But you have to eat," I told her. "You'll get sick!"

"I *am* sick," said Minnow, and she went to bed.

"What's wrong now?" I asked Alice. "Do you think I should take her temperature?"

"Oh, leave her alone!" said Alice. "It takes more than skip-ping one meal to starve."

Alice went back to the sofa to get on with *Caddie Wood-lawn*. Since she wasn't limping as much, I assumed she would sleep upstairs with me, but she refused. She obviously intended to read all night, so I went to bed alone.

Around one o'clock the next morning, a storm hit the island. And I mean really hit, as if some giant had taken a club and swung it at us. The house gave a sudden shake, and there was a rumble of thunder. All the shutters rattled, and the rain hit the windowpanes like firecrackers going off on the Fourth of

July. I reached for the light switch, but it didn't work. There was no electricity.

Although I adore storms, Minnow doesn't. I padded down the hall to reassure her, but her bed was empty. Holding tight to the bannister, I felt my way down the stairs to see if she was with Alice. I have a tendency to lose my balance in the dark.

Over the noise of the storm, a voice was wailing, "*Come, night; come, Romeo; come, thou day in night!*"

I pushed open the living room door. "Is Minnow with you, Juliet?"

"Hi, Legs!" said Alice. "What a beautiful storm!"

"Gorgeous," I agreed. "Where's Minnow?"

"I don't know," said Alice. "Hiding under the covers, most likely."

"Her bed is empty," I told her. "Help me find a flashlight!"

But Alice was off again:

"*Come, gentle night; come, loving, black-brow'd night,*
Give me my Romeo – "

I closed the door.

We had used up the candle stubs our first night, when we sat around the table eating crackers. All I could find were the kitchen matches. Burning them one by one, I searched the house for Minnow. The thunder grew even louder, and the lightning was blinding when it lit up the sky. I thought I'd find Minnow hiding in a closet, but instead, I found her in the bathroom, throwing up.

"Minnow, honey!" I said, putting my arm around her shoulder. "The storm won't hurt you."

She was sick again. All of a sudden, I was frightened. Not because of the storm, but because it struck me that Minnow might have eaten something really bad. What if a piece of amanita had slipped in with the chanterelles? I didn't feel sick

73

myself, and Alice was obviously in good form, but what if Minnow had gotten the poisonous piece? She might die!

"Wait here!" I told her. "Don't move. I'm going to call Dr. Pierce."

I nearly fell downstairs as I ran to the phone, but it was no use. The phone wasn't working, either. I scrambled upstairs, in a real panic.

"Where does it hurt, Minnow?" I asked. "Do you feel delirious or anything? What did you eat, do you remember?"

Minnow was too sick to answer.

"Oh, Minnow!" I wailed. "I don't want you to die! Please don't die, Minnow! Oh, I hope I never see another mushroom in my life!"

Minnow sat back and groped for a towel to wipe her mouth. There was another flash of lightning, and for a moment, I could see her face. It was very pale, but it looked alive enough.

"I'm better now," she said. "It wasn't mushrooms."

"How do you know?" I asked.

"I didn't eat any," said Minnow. "I didn't eat *anything* for supper, remember?"

I nearly fainted from relief. "What made you so sick, then?"

At first, Minnow wouldn't tell me. She followed me back to my room and got in bed with me, still shivering. I rubbed her feet a little, to warm her up.

"You'd better tell me," I said. "I won't get mad, I promise. But I think I ought to know."

Minnow hesitated. Then she confessed. "Pepperoni."

"Pepperoni?" I repeated. "Alice's pepperoni? I thought it was all gone by now."

"Well, there was a whole stick left," said Minnow. "I found it under the socks, with *Caddie Woodlawn*."

"So *that's* what took you so long!" I said. "How much of it did you eat?"

"All of it," said Minnow.

"But I thought you *hated* pepperoni!" I protested. "You know spicy food makes you sick. What on earth made you do it?"

Minnow yawned and snuggled down under the covers. "I thought I'd die if I had to eat any more survival," she told me sleepily. "Survival is for the birds!"

CHAPTER SIX

I had a bad night.

The excitement of thinking Minnow had eaten a poisoned mushroom kept me jittery for hours, and when I started to calm down, the electricity went on, so I had to get up to turn my light off. Then Minnow kept trying to lie crossways over the bed, with her feet jabbing into my stomach. After she fell asleep, I moved into Alice's empty bed and lay there listening to the wind and rain die down, until at last all I could hear were those two foghorns mooing drearily, the cow and the calf.

It was growing light outside by the time I dozed off, and I couldn't have slept more than a few minutes before Minnow sat bolt upright with a loud creaking of the bedsprings.

"Allegra!" she announced. "I forgot to tell you. I'm out of school glue!"

I had been dreaming that I was in a Baskin-Robbins ice

cream store. There were a hundred and forty-eight different flavors, but I kept saying that all I wanted was periwinkle. Periwinkle ice cream! I couldn't get the man at the counter to understand me because the whole time Alice was yelling, "*Come, night! come, Romeo.*" It wasn't exactly a nightmare, but it wasn't one of my better dreams, either.

When Minnow made her announcement about school glue, it fitted into my dream because the man handed me a double-dip, school-glue cone with sprinkles on top. Then the cone vanished and was replaced by Minnow in her pink nightie.

"You woke me up!" I accused her.

"It's an emergency," said Minnow. "I'm all out of school glue."

"That's the least of your problems," I told her. "When Alice finds out you ate her last stick of pepperoni, she'll mash *you* into school glue."

"Alice never gets mad," said Minnow. But she didn't sound convinced.

It was chilly that morning. The storm had cleared the air, and even though the sun sparkled on the waves out in the bay, a cold wind blew through the window. I slammed the window shut and jumped back into bed to warm up.

Minnow and I lay there talking about one thing and another. There was no reason to dress and go downstairs because there was nothing to eat for breakfast, unless you counted the leftover wild salad.

We were just discussing what we would order for breakfast if we were in a hotel, when we heard footsteps racing upstairs. They proved that Alice was only pretending about her ankle the night before. No one who is in mortal agony one day could take the stairs three at a time the next.

I had moved Alice's unpacked suitcase out to the hall, and

now I could hear her rummaging in it. There was a moment of silence, followed by a shriek of rage.

"What do you think is the matter?" asked Minnow, who knew perfectly well what the matter was.

I smiled. "Why should you care? Alice never gets mad, right?"

We were obviously about to find out. Minnow dived under the covers just as Alice threw open the door and shouted, "Okay, guys! What did you do with it?"

I didn't answer, but Alice could tell by my face that I was innocent. "Where's Minnow?" she demanded.

The lump under the covers flattened out.

"You rat!" Alice roared, tearing the covers off the bed. "That was my last piece, and I was going to have some for breakfast."

Minnow pulled her head into her nightgown like a turtle in its shell.

"She was sick all night," I said. "No use crying over spilled milk, Alice."

"Milk!" Alice screamed. "Milk! I put up with a lot, but this is the limit. That stick of pepperoni was all that was left between me and starvation. Find me some milk, and I'll forgive her!"

A frightened little voice squeaked out from under Minnow's nightgown. "If there had been any milk, I wouldn't have needed your disgusting pepperoni."

I could hear five successive doors slam as Alice stamped out of the house.

"You're safe now," I told Minnow. "She'll wander around feeling sorry for herself until she decides what Juliet would have had to say about it. So could you please let me get some sleep?"

I must have dozed for another hour or so. When I woke up again, the foghorns had stopped, and the white-throated sparrows were singing like crazy out in the fir trees. It was still chilly, and I pulled on two sweaters before I went downstairs.

Alice was nowhere to be seen, but Minnow sat at the kitchen table admiring the percolator, which she had just finished covering with shells. There was one big periwinkle pasted to the glass knob on the lid, and a whole line of little ones around the handle. It looked weird. I didn't think it would be convenient to pick up, much less make coffee in. But what really caught my attention was the white smear on Minnow's face.

"I thought you ran out of school glue," I said. "Did you find some more?"

"I *made* some more," said Minnow. "Allegra, how about if I do a frying pan next? Do you think I should put the shells on the inside or the outside?"

"Neither," I said. "How did you make glue?"

"Flour and water, of course," said Minnow. "We learned at school. I know what, Allegra. How about if I paste shells all over the toilet seat in Mummy and Daddy's bathroom, the way some people have furry pink covers, you know?"

"I wouldn't," I advised her. "Where did you find the flour, Minnow?"

"In the storeroom, of course," said Minnow. "On the top shelf, where it always is."

"Why on earth didn't you tell me when we were looking for food?" I cried. "We could have *used* flour!"

"I *am* using it," said Minnow, licking her fingers. "I need it for my projects."

I guarded that flour like the crown jewels. Minnow was furious, but I didn't give in. I kept the cannister locked up in my suitcase and wore the key on a string around my neck. The first thing I made with the flour was pancakes.

"Run get me the cookbook, Minnow," I said. "I'm fixing breakfast."

"How about shells on the cookbook cover?" Minnow asked. "That would look pretty!"

I rubbed my stomach. "How about pancakes, Minnow?"

That got her. She ran for the book, and I found what I wanted under "Griddlecakes and Waffles."

"Eggs, milk, butter," I read aloud. "We don't have any of that stuff. I'll just have to keep it simple."

Simple it was. I mixed flour, water, sugar, and a pinch of salt. Minnow watched. At first, I thought she wanted to learn to cook, but when she objected to the salt and sugar because the mixture might not glue as well, I knew what she was up to. My sisters have one-track minds.

"We're going to eat this, Minnow," I reminded her, "not just smear it on a coffee can."

"How are you going to cook it?" Minnow asked.

That was another problem. I looked in the book again. "It says to rub the frying pan with a cut turnip. I wonder why? Mummy just puts in a little oil."

"What's a turnip?" asked Minnow.

"I think people used to make soap out of them in the olden days," I told her.

It really was a crazy, old-fashioned book. I put it back on the shelf and made the pancakes my own way. They were heavy and kind of sticky because I didn't cook them enough, but after four days of us living off the land, they tasted good. Minnow and I gobbled up a dozen of them before we felt full enough to stop.

"Alice doesn't know what she's missing!" I said when we were through. "Where do you suppose she is?"

Minnow shrugged. "I don't know. She never came back."

I went down to the beach to look for her, but Alice wasn't there. The tide was dead low, and I gathered a few periwinkles, but I didn't bother to get too many because I was planning pancakes again for lunch and supper.

"Alice!" I called from time to time.

My voice sounded like one more sea gull. No one answered, so I walked around the bluff to the next beach. When Alice is feeling more than ordinarily romantic, she'll walk there sometimes, but that beach was deserted, too.

"Did Alice come home yet?" I asked when I got back to the house.

Minnow shook her head.

"It's not like her to bear a grudge," I commented. "I hope she didn't wander off and get lost or something."

I wasn't really concerned yet because Alice was thirteen. Even though she was perfectly capable of getting lost, it wouldn't panic her the way it would Minnow. I borrowed *Caddie Woodlawn* and read it outside on the grass until it was time for lunch.

The second batch of pancakes turned out better than the first because I remembered to cook them longer.

"If we keep this up, we may even put on weight," I told Minnow cheerfully. "Aren't they delicious?"

"They're not as bad as survival," said Minnow, "but a little maple syrup would hide the pasty taste."

"I thought you liked the taste of paste!" I said crossly. "You should be the last person to complain."

I put a few pancakes aside for Alice and looked anxiously at the clock. "It's going on three," I told Minnow. "It couldn't have been later than eight when Alice left the house. She's been gone for seven hours!"

Minnow yelled outside, all around the house. Then we both walked to the point where we had made our church on Sunday. We could see for miles down the shore, but there was no sign of Alice. In a way, that was a relief because I was afraid she had fallen off a rock again and hit her head.

"Maybe she went to look for chanterelles," I told Minnow. "Let's go down the road and shout into the woods."

We walked all the way to the mailbox, shouting our heads off, but still no answer. I tried hard not to panic. Something was always going wrong! That morning I had been thinking how lucky we were that the electricity was back on, and that Minnow didn't have mushroom poisoning, and that Alice's ankle was all better. We even had flour to cook with, so our worries were over. And then what happens? I lose a sister.

"Hey, look!" said Minnow, opening the mailbox. "There's a postcard."

It was from Aunt Ruth, and I read it aloud: "Having a pleasant time in Quebec. Friend much improved. Love to all of you, and a special hug for little Edith."

"We'd better get rid of it," I said, slipping it into my pocket. "Little Edith is supposed to be in Belfast."

Minnow scowled and started to say what she thought of being called Edith. I hushed her up. "Wait!" I said. "Do you hear what I hear?"

A faraway voice, faint but clear, was calling:
"Wilt thou be gone? it is not yet near day:
It was the nightingale, and not the lark . . ."
"That's Shakespeare!" I said.
"No, it's not," said Minnow. "It's Alice."
The wailing grew closer:
"Nightly she sings on yon pomegranate tree:
Believe me, love, it was the nightingale."
"Alice!" I shouted. "Where on earth have you been?"
Alice came around the corner, carrying an armful of books. "Hi, Legs! I went to the library. I turned in your Nancy Drews

and took out some of the books on my summer reading list."

"But I never got a chance to read my Nancy Drews!" I protested.

Then it struck me what she had done. "You mean you walked all the way back to the library? Seven miles in and seven miles back? What for?"

"There was nothing left to read," said Alice. "I finished *Caddie Woodlawn* last night."

I was furious. I told Alice how worried I had been. Wild animals might have devoured her, for all I knew. I told her how stupid it was to walk fourteen miles on her sprained ankle. Besides, somebody might have recognized her and telephoned our parents. I also told her what I thought of someone who turns in her sister's Nancy Drews before her sister gets a chance to read them.

Alice just smiled. She pulled a big stick of pepperoni from her pocket and bit into it.

I stopped preaching. "Wherever did you get *that* from?"

"I bought it at Waterman's," said Alice.

"Bought it with what?" I demanded.

"With the money Daddy gave us for the five-and-dime," said Alice.

I tried hard not to strangle her. "But the money was for all of us! What else did you buy?"

"More pepperoni," said Alice.

That set me off again. I called her a no-good, double-crossing, self-centered pig, but she just offered me a bite of pepperoni. Alice is impossible. After a while, I got tired of yelling and gave up.

"Are you sure nobody recognized you?" I asked her.

"I was really careful," said Alice. "As soon as I got close to town, I disguised myself."

She showed me a pair of purple pixie sunglasses with rhinestones on the frame, and my father's sou'wester. I made her put them on, to see. Alice was completely unrecognizable with those silly glasses under the big yellow hat, but she certainly looked weird.

"They must have thought you were cuckoo," I said. "You're lucky they didn't lock you up."

It was high tide when we got home, so we changed into our suits and went for a swim. For a dunk, to be truthful – we didn't actually swim because the water seemed ten degrees colder after the storm. Then we walked along the beach to warm up again, looking at all the new things the storm had brought in the night before.

The beaches on North Haven are mostly stones, not sand. Storm waves had washed the stones into high, unfamiliar ridges, strewn with kelp and driftwood and a scattering of plastic bottles. Minnow found a dead cuttlefish that stared at us with a glassy eye. Alice found a lobster buoy, tangled into a long green rope. I picked up a few pieces of sea glass that had grown smooth and frosty from grinding with the stones.

"Aren't we lucky to be here?" I asked my sisters. "All three of us safe and sound, and no Aunt Ruth? And only two more days until Mummy and Daddy come home. Let's hope nothing bad happens between now and then!"

Alice and Minnow stared at me and said together, "What could happen?" Then they both giggled.

I could have screamed, I felt so impatient with them. Neither seemed to have the slightest sense of self-preservation. I was frightened to death that there would be some terrible accident before my parents got back. For a moment, I was tempted to tether them to a stake on the lawn, like a pair of goats. Then I sighed and shrugged.

"Never mind. I'm freezing. Who wants to go back up to the house and have another look for the treasure?"

"No, thanks," Alice said in a bored voice. "I'm all treasured out."

"I've looked all over my room," said Minnow.

"Big deal!" I said. "There's still the whole rest of the house. At the rate we're going, we'll never find it on time."

"There's nothing to find," said Alice. "That secret panel business is ridiculous – we don't have a panel-type house. And if it were hidden anywhere else, we would have found it years ago. I know every inch of that house by heart. Don't you, Legs?"

I agreed. "It might not really be hidden, though. I mean, it may just be stashed in some place with a lot of other junk, so we never noticed it."

Minnow squealed. "Oh, like the diamonds might be mixed in with some costume jewelry in a trunk in the attic!"

"Well, not exactly," I said. "We don't keep any costume jewelry in the attic. We don't even keep trunks up there."

Alice had been skipping flat stones across the water. She stopped suddenly and spun around. "Yes, we do. There's somebody's old camp trunk filled with books and magazines and stuff. Maybe I'll find something good to read!"

The attic was nice and warm, even after the storm. We found some old books, and a kite that we thought we had lost long ago, and a lot of mouse droppings, but no treasure. Alice took a stepladder and felt up around the eaves, but she tore her fingernail on a nail and gave up in disgust.

"I tell you, the only treasure in this house is something dumb like a box of peanut brittle, and it won't even be here until Thursday," she said. "We're wasting our time."

"Anyway," I said, "it must be nearly suppertime, and I've got a good idea for a recipe."

"You can eat it yourself, then," said Alice. "Today, I'm having a vacation from feasting my way to survival."

I guessed from her smug expression that she meant the half-eaten stick of pepperoni in her pocket.

"But, Alice, we're not having survival for supper. We're having pancakes!" said Minnow.

Alice's jaw dropped. "Pancakes? Are you kidding?"

"What's it to you?" I asked. "You can go off and make a hog of yourself over that repulsive sausage."

"It'll keep," said Alice happily. "Tonight, I'll just have pancakes."

Not a word about where the pancakes came from – she didn't know and didn't care. She probably thought they dropped from heaven, or came in the mail. Alice is so impractical!

I got to work on my recipe, which was fried periwinkles. First, I boiled them, and then I picked them all out with a pin. It took forever, but did anyone offer to help me? Not on your life. Alice took a hot bath with a library book, and Minnow wandered around the house in the pixie sunglasses and my father's sou'wester, singing the doxology.

When I cornered Minnow and asked her to give me a hand, she said, "No thanks, Allegra," and sat down to watch.

Just as I was rolling the periwinkle bodies in flour and salt, a truck drove up outside the house. Terrified, I rushed around pulling shutters closed as fast as I could and locked the kitchen door. Then I raced upstairs to the bathroom, dragging Minnow after me.

"Is it murdering thieves, Allegra?" gasped Minnow. "Tell me the truth. Is it murdering thieves?"

"I don't know, and I'm not going to find out," I panted.

Luckily, Alice had left the bathroom door open. I shoved

Minnow inside and locked it behind us. "Now, even if they do get into the house, we're safe," I said.

"Who's getting into the house?" Alice asked, looking up from her book with only the mildest interest.

"We've got visitors," I told her. "Didn't you hear the truck?"

"The water was running," said Alice, and she turned a page.

I grabbed the book away from her. "Pay attention, Alice! Somebody just drove up. Did we leave anything on the lawn?"

"Not on the lawn," said Alice. "Just our bathing suits on the line. Give back my book, Allegra!"

"Are you crazy?" I said. "Don't you understand? We're in trouble! Who can it be?"

Alice lay back and trailed her fingers dreamily in the bath water, but Minnow stuck her thumb in her mouth – a thing I hadn't seen her do for years. I held her on my lap and listened hard. Judging by the voices, there were at least two men outside.

"Thugs?" asked Minnow.

"Nonsense!" I said. "It's more likely the police, come after Alice. They followed her home, and now they're going to take her away to a lunatic asylum."

"Really?" said Alice, paying attention at last. "Are they armed? Is the house surrounded?"

She had been reading too much Nancy Drew. "Oh, shut up!" I said crossly. "Let's lie low and hope they go away, whoever it is. And let's hope they don't notice our bathing suits. Even if it's just the man about the electric meter, he might make trouble."

Minnow took her thumb out of her mouth and looked at me with a pitying expression on her face. "You worry too much, Allegra. You shouldn't worry so much."

"If I didn't worry, we might all be dead," I told her.

"No, we wouldn't," said Alice. "We'd be in Boston."

She lunged for her book, splashing water all over me and Minnow. I was about to splash her back when suddenly there was a terrible racket outside. I thought it was a machine gun until I recognized the sound – it was a buzz saw.

We were all relieved. Nobody who came to a lonely house with evil intent, as they say in mystery stories, would make a noise like that.

I unlocked the bathroom door and crept down the hall to a window that looked out over the front of the house. Standing well to the side so no one could see me, I pushed the shutter open just an inch and peeked out.

A red pickup truck was parked where the driveway ended. Next to it, two men had dumped a pile of logs and were sawing them into smaller pieces. It was just Calvin Moon, Dickie Moon's husband, and his son Bert. I remembered that my father had said we were out of firewood. Calvin was delivering some more.

It took those men two hours to saw the pile of logs. In fact, they didn't even finish. They seemed to be having some kind of party while they were at it. Bert's big transistor radio was tuned to a country music station, and there were two six-packs of beer. Bert sawed while Calvin sat down and guzzled beer. Then Calvin had a turn with the saw while Bert guzzled. It was exasperating. We were still scared to death they would come into the house, so we kept as quiet as mice. Alice's bath grew cold. She got out and dressed again, but we didn't dare pull the plug in the tub in case the water made a noise. It was getting dark by the time the men stacked the logs in the woodpile and drove away.

"Thank goodness!" said Alice. "Now we can turn on the lights and eat supper."

I ran out to bring in the bathing suits. They were still on the line, flapping in the wind and already beginning to get damp again in the evening dew.

"It's lucky they're dark colors," I thought to myself. "They don't show up much against the trees. It's lucky we didn't choose shocking pink."

It occurred to me that we had been depending a lot on luck that week, in spite of all my organization. I could hardly wait until my parents came back to take over some of the responsibilities.

Our food problems seemed to have lessened, at any rate. The fried periwinkles were delicious. I made an orach salad, and we sprinkled sugar on our pancakes. For once, we went to bed on happy stomachs.

"What would Aunt Ruth say?" Alice asked as we went upstairs. "Do you realize that we didn't eat until nine and now it's midnight? And I'm still going to read until I fall asleep."

At first, I didn't object because it was nice to have Alice back in my room again, but it was impossible to sleep with the light on.

"Alice!" I whispered after a while.

She turned a page. "Go to sleep, Legs. It's really late. You'll be exhausted in the morning."

"Speak for yourself," I said. "Couldn't you at least drape a T-shirt over the lamp or something so it isn't so bright?"

Alice dropped her book on the floor and reached for the switch.

"Yon light is not daylight, I know it, I:
It is some meteor that the sun exhales,
To be to thee this night a torchbearer
And light thee on thy way to Mantua."

"It *will* be daylight soon, and I'm tired!" I complained.

But Alice had decided it was a good time to run through the balcony scene, so I pulled the pillow over my head until I fell asleep.

CHAPTER SEVEN

The shutters on the front of the house had been closed all week. The next morning, I left the ones on the bay side closed, too, all but a tiny crack. It was so dark and chilly inside that I made myself some hot tea and took it out into the sunlight. I wanted to make sure we hadn't left anything lying around to show we were there.

We had. I found a paring knife, a book that Alice had been reading on the grass and that was now all puffed up from the dew, and a pair of Minnow's underpants. Minnow has a terrible habit of leaving her underpants wherever she goes. Someday, I'll have to break her of it. As for the paring knife, I guess that was my fault. But nobody's perfect.

"Let's get away from here today," I said when my sisters turned up for breakfast. "What if Bert and Calvin come back to finish sawing that wood? Let's lock up and spend the day on the picnic beach."

The picnic beach is three coves down. The only way to get to it is by walking along the shore, and there is some tricky rock-climbing on the way. Once you arrive, it's heaven – just a baby cove with steep rocks all around, so it's hidden from sight unless a boat goes by. Usually, my sisters would have jumped at the idea of going there, but today, they just looked bored.

"It's a long walk, Legs," said Alice. "Anyway, the tide will be dead low at lunchtime."

"So what?" I said. "It's easier to get to at low tide, and look who's complaining about long walks! You walked all the way to town and back yesterday, just for a stick of pepperoni."

"That's why I'm tired today," said Alice. "I'm going to stay home and read."

"Besides, what about the treasure?" asked Minnow. "I was planning to dig in the garden for it this morning. A lot of people bury their gold in their gardens."

"What gold?" I asked. "What garden?"

My father had once suggested starting a vegetable garden. He liked the idea of growing our own string beans instead of paying for them by the piece at Waterman's. But my mother just said that she was on vacation in North Haven, and if he wanted a garden he could plant it himself.

"There might have been a garden, once upon a time," said Minnow.

"No digging!" said Alice. "I've tried digging, and it's harder than you think."

I threw her a dirty look and changed the subject fast. "You know what? This will be the first time we've ever been alone to the picnic beach. It may be the last time, too. I'll make the lunch, okay? And I promise I'll carry it."

Minnow gave in, and after I reminded her that she could

bring a book along, Alice gave in, too. I got busy making sand-wiches.

It was a good thing we had so much flour; there was no need to ration the pancakes. I made us two big pancake sandwiches apiece for our picnic – one with orach leaves inside, and one with sugar. Our sugar supply was getting low, but my parents would be coming back the next day, so it didn't matter.

"Do you both have your bathing suits?" I asked. "Don't for-get your book, Alice! And Minnow, if you're going to lose your underpants again, you might as well not wear any."

We finally got everything together in a big canvas bag, and Alice was nice enough to take turns carrying it with me, in-stead of reminding me of my promise. The house looked tidy and snug when we left it. I didn't think Bert and Calvin would notice a thing.

Alice and I walked along the water's edge to the beach be-cause it isn't easy to climb unless you have both hands free. It isn't easy to walk on wet, slippery seaweed, either, but at least it's fairly flat.

Having nothing to carry, Minnow scrambled up and down the rocks above us like a mountain goat. She got way ahead, and when Alice and I finally rounded the last point, she was already sitting on the picnic beach. All she had on were her plastic sandals and a kelp "lion's tail" tied around her waist and trailing down behind.

I groaned. "Where are your underpants, Minnow?"

Minnow pointed behind her. "I put them there so I'd be sure not to forget."

She had left her jeans and T-shirt folded neatly on a rock, but her underpants were hanging like a flag from a driftwood branch.

"Well, just so you don't go and lose them again," I said. "Where's your bathing suit?"

"I don't need one," said Minnow.

You didn't on a beach like that. There wasn't a boat in sight except for a couple of schooners, way out in the bay. Even if a boat did come by, there were rocks to hide behind if you really cared.

The tide was too low for good swimming, but it was so hot that we decided to go in anyway. I left my clothes on the rock with Minnow's. Even Alice forgot her dignity and swam naked. She started out with a suit, but when she realized how silly she looked next to me and Minnow, she peeled it off and threw it high up the beach.

The water was fairly warm for Maine. Usually, you just dash in and out, shrieking, but that day, we stayed in and fooled around. I'm not as frightened of underwater things when I'm with the others, so I stuck close to Minnow, and we had a seaweed war, heaving huge clumps of it at each other. I splashed and yelled as if I were seven, too. I hadn't had such a good time all week.

"Grow up, Legs!" said Alice when a clump of seaweed smacked her in the face.

I just laughed, and Alice waded away, muttering, "*O serpent heart, hid with a flowering face!*"

She tossed her head, looked up at the sky with an anguished expression, tripped, and fell into the water. When she sat up, there was seaweed on her nose.

"You look good with a flowering face," I told her.

"Oh, shut up, Allegra!" said Alice.

It's a bad sign when she calls me Allegra. I left Minnow and waded over to Alice. "Did you get hurt?"

She shook her head. "I fell on seaweed. It's soft."

"It's too shallow here," I said. "Let's swim out to that lobster buoy."

Alice looked at the buoy appraisingly. It was a red and white one, bobbing in the water about twenty yards away. "It's too far. We'll freeze!"

"No, we won't," I said. "The water's warm today. Come on, I dare you!"

"I will if you go first," said Alice.

I swam out to the buoy, touched it, and turned back in a hurry. My heart beat harder as I imagined all those lobsters snapping at my toes under the water. "There!" I said, shivering. "Now you do it."

"Oh, all right," she grumbled.

Alice is too absentminded to worry about things snapping at her toes. She swam out lazily. My teeth started chattering, so I went to get my clothes. After pulling on my jeans and T-shirt, I ran up the beach a little to warm up. When I came back, Alice was floating around out by the lobster buoy, crooning:

"*O Romeo, Romeo! wherefore art thou Romeo?*

Deny thy father, and refuse thy name;

Or, if thou wilt not, be but sworn my love..."

I walked down to the water's edge and stared at her. "Alice, you nut! You'll turn into an ice cube."

"It doesn't feel cold anymore," she called back.

"That's the first sign of frostbite, dummy!" I shouted.

But Alice just splashed happily. "*'Tis but thy name that is my enemy.*"

"Do you think she's lost her mind?" I asked Minnow. "Or is she just showing off?"

"I hear a boat," said Minnow.

Minnow has good ears. There was a muffled putt-putt

sound coming around the point. "Alice!" I yelled, pulling Minnow behind a rock.

But Alice was yelling even louder:

"What's in a name? that which we call a rose
By any other name would smell as sweet – "

Then she saw the boat. It was one of those fancy motor launches, with two couples dressed to the teeth in the kind of silly boating clothes that so far I had only seen in mail-order catalogs. They were staring at Alice as if she had escaped from a zoo. Alice turned bright red. From the chin up, that is. The rest of her was probably blue, but being naked, she kept it underwater.

"It's a mermaid!" said one of the men, and the women giggled.

Alice looked more like a particularly deadly kind of jellyfish. Her blond hair was floating all around her like tentacles, and there was still a piece of seaweed on her head.

"Hello, sweetheart!" said the other man. "Want a ride?"

"No," said Alice.

The boat moved in slow circles while the people teased, and joked, and asked questions. They wanted to know who she was and how she had gotten there. Alice made it up as she went along – she was smart enough not to let out any secrets – but her teeth were chattering, and the people wouldn't leave.

"What's the name of this island?" one of the women asked.

"North Haven," said Alice.

I thought they must be pretty dumb if they didn't even know where they were, but it was a relief to be sure they were strangers.

"What are we going to do?" I asked Minnow. "Alice will freeze if they don't go away."

"I have an idea," said Minnow. She ran out from behind the rock with her kelp tail flapping around her bare, white bottom. It would never occur to Minnow to worry about being naked. Anyway, when you're seven, it doesn't matter.

"Here's your bathing suit, Alice!" she shouted. "Put it on underwater, and you can come back."

She threw a soggy, dark-green bundle toward Alice, but it didn't get anywhere near her. Instead, it landed with a plop in the shallow water a few yards away from where I was standing. I was already in my jeans again and didn't feel like wading out to rescue the suit, and Alice was too modest to swim closer to shore where the water was transparent.

There was a moment of silence before the couples in the boat burst out laughing.

"Poor kid!" said one of the men. "Let's leave her to her misery." He turned up the motor, and the boat roared away, leaving a wake that nearly drowned Alice.

As soon as the boat was out of sight, Alice dashed out of the water. She didn't wait to put on her suit. Her skin was purple, and she was shivering so hard that when she tried to talk, she bit her tongue.

"That damn boat!" she kept saying. "Those damn people!"

I rubbed her back with our only towel. "Serves you right! If you hadn't been yelling all that nonsense about roses, you'd have heard them coming."

We ate our picnic as soon as Alice's hands were warm enough to hold a pancake sandwich. No more boats went by, but even Minnow was a little bored with nudity. She pulled on her jeans and threaded the kelp tail through the belt loop over her behind. Then she followed me down to the water's edge to pull up some mussels. I planned to roll them in flour and fry them like the periwinkles for supper.

"Watch out for barnacles!" I warned Minnow. "And don't slip on the seaweed."

Minnow stooped to twist a large mussel out of its bed, then straightened up. "I'm not doing this," she announced. "I'm sick of cleaning mussels."

"Out of my way, then," I said. "You're splashing me."

Daintily hooking up her kelp tail as if she were a lady in long skirts, Minnow picked her way along the shore and climbed partway up the steep rocks at the side of the cove.

"I can still see those people's boat," she called down to me. "They're headed for Camden." Holding her tail with one hand, she waved at the boat with the other.

"Don't let go!" I yelled. "You'll slip!"

"Don't what?" asked Minnow, and turning to see me better, she slipped.

I could practically hear the barnacles scraping her skin on the way down; Minnow was wearing jeans, but no shirt. Then I saw her back and screamed. It was a gory mess.

"It doesn't hurt, Allegra," said Minnow. "Don't start worrying again."

I splashed a little water on her and looked a second time. Actually, she had only a few scratches; the squashed seaweed had looked like blood at first. But I was a nervous wreck.

"Let's go home," I said. "I can't take any more accidents."

Minnow raised her eyebrows. "Nothing has happened to *you*, Allegra!"

"I'm going to have a nervous breakdown when this week is over, that's all," I told her. "Run put on your shirt."

The tide was coming in again by the time we were packed up and ready to start for home. We had to carry the bag over the rocks, and it was slow going. When we finally climbed to the top of the first point, we sat down for a final glimpse of the picnic beach below us.

"Oh, no!" wailed Minnow.

"What?" I asked.

I looked where she was pointing. There were Minnow's underpants, waving on the driftwood branch. I could just make out the little yellow flowers.

"That's rather sweet!" said Alice. "It's like planting the American flag on the moon – claiming our territory!"

"Tell that to Mummy when she gets home," I said crossly. "I'm not going back to get them, Minnow. And I think you're ridiculous!"

"Who needs underpants?" asked Minnow. She scampered down the rocks to the next cove.

As soon as we got home, I hung up Alice's suit in the kitchen so no one would see it drying on the line, and made sure my sisters hadn't left their sandals on the lawn, and checked that all the shutters were still closed.

"You're silly, Legs," said Alice. "No one is going to come."

"Bert and Calvin never finished sawing that wood," I reminded her. "I don't want to spoil our last day."

"But I wanted to read!" she argued.

I refused to give in. "Read outside, then. Just listen for car motors, and when you come back in, don't leave your book on the lawn."

"Oh, forget it," said Alice. "Where's the trowel, Minnow? We might try digging around the birdbath. People who bury treasure outside always put it near some landmark so they won't forget."

I glared at her. "What's the big idea? You don't believe in the treasure in the first place, so why get her hopes up?"

Alice just laughed and danced out across the lawn, fencing with the trowel and shouting out Romeo's lines from the duel in the third act.

"Don't mess up the lawn!" I shouted. "If Calvin Moon comes back, he's sure to notice freshly-dug earth."

Actually, it turned out I made all that fuss for nothing. No one came, but I felt nervous anyway. Once, the telephone rang, and I jumped a mile in the air. It's a funny feeling to let a telephone keep ringing when you can't pick up the receiver. It seems to go on forever.

"I wonder who that was?" Minnow called from outside.

Alice's answer was faint but clear. "Thieves. That's how they check to see if a house is empty. If no one answers, they know it's safe to come."

"You idiot!" I shouted. "Haven't you got something better to do than scare Minnow?"

Alice came back inside, followed by Minnow, whose thumb was back in her mouth. "No," she said. "There's nothing that could even begin to be gold pieces out there. There are plenty of worms, though. How come we haven't tried fishing?"

I was too worried about the telephone call to think about fishing. "I wonder if it was Mummy and Daddy?" I said. "Do you suppose they had some way of tracing my calls and found out I was telephoning from the island?"

"We should probably call them again," said Alice. "If they keep calling Aunt Ruth's number and nobody answers, they'll start to worry."

I knew she was right. In fact, I was afraid they had already started to worry. After all, they hadn't heard from us since Saturday. What if they had found out we never went to Aunt Ruth's and were frantically trying to track us down? Half of me wanted to set their minds at rest, but the other half wanted to take the chance they didn't know yet, and put off the trouble for one more day.

"Let's think about it," I said. "Maybe I'll call later tonight – only they're going to smell something fishy if I tell them Aunt Ruth can't come to the phone again."

I sent Minnow out to pick raspberries while I cleaned the mussels, scraping them into the sink for once because there were so few. I steamed them, picked them all out, rolled them in flour, and fried them in hot oil.

"Mussels are a pain!" I announced.

"Women's work is never done," said Alice, looking over my shoulder.

"Guess why?" I said. "Can't you help?"

"Okay," said Alice. But she didn't.

When Minnow came back with the berries, I made raspberry pancakes for supper. By the time they were eaten, it was dark.

"Bert and Calvin would never come so late," said Alice. "Can't we open the shutters now?"

"What for?" I asked. "It's dark outside."

"That makes it even worse," said Alice. "It feels all closed up in here, and I'm too hot."

I gave in and opened one pair of shutters in the kitchen, after turning off the light so the bugs wouldn't come in. The three of us leaned out and looked into the night. There was a full moon shining on the water, and the spruce trees threw long moon-shadows across the lawn.

"What are all those funny lights?" asked Minnow.

"Fireflies," said Alice.

"Not those," said Minnow. "I mean down on the water."

From time to time there was a splash, followed by a frosty patch of light on the water's surface.

"Oh, that's phosphorescence," I said. "You know, Daddy showed you. You throw in a stone, and the water glows."

"Who's down there throwing stones?" asked Minnow.

"No one, silly," I said. "It's just fish jumping or something, out in the bay."

"Let's go outside!" said Alice suddenly.

"Now?" I asked. "It's late!"

Alice shrugged. "Who cares? There's a full moon. Let's go throw stones in the water. Come on, Legs! You said we could do whatever we wanted."

I regretted ever having spoken those words. "We'll get eaten up."

"Not if we put on mosquito lotion," said Alice.

We could see perfectly well from the kitchen window, but getting down to the beach through the trees was another matter. None of the moonlight filtered to the path. I went first, groping my way along with Minnow holding on to my belt loop, so close behind that she kept stepping on my ankles.

Alice trailed along after, bumping into things and muttering, "*O! swear not by the moon, the inconstant moon.*"

"Isn't it funny?" I said. "When you can't see, you smell better."

"You don't smell better to *me*," said Alice.

I ignored her. "I can smell pine needles, and wild bay leaves, and raspberries, and salt."

"Salt doesn't have any smell," said Minnow.

"You know what I mean, dummy," I told her.

"Well, all I can smell is Ajax," said Minnow, stepping on my heel. "You must have used too much on the frying pan."

"How can you smell all those things, Legs?" asked Alice. "I only smell mosquito lotion. And it's not working."

"I *told* you we'd be eaten up," I said. "What a dumb idea!" Nevertheless, we went all the way down to the beach. The mosquitoes weren't so bad down there, and it was fun throwing stones into the bay. The glowing pools of phosphorescence would swell up and fade away, and once, a whole school of fish slapped around on the surface of the water. It was exciting being there alone in the moonlight, just the three of us. In fact, for a moment, I wished the week weren't nearly over.

"Only one more day," I said. "And we got through alive."

"Let's hope we're still alive after Mummy and Daddy find out about this," said Alice. "We're going to have a lot of explaining to do. Have you thought of that yet, Legs?"

I had been thinking all evening, and the more I thought, the guiltier I felt. "The big problem is tomorrow morning," I said. "They'll want to make arrangements for meeting us in Rockland. They might even drive to Belfast to pick us up."

"They'll be furious!" Alice commented unnecessarily.

"There are two things," I continued. "One is us staying here alone – they might not get too mad about that if we can convince them we were responsible and everything. But the other is making them worry, and they're not going to like that at all."

"Well, it was your idea," said Alice. "You got us into this mess, Allegra, so it's up to you to get us out of it."

I don't know which is worse, feeling guilty or feeling angry. In any case, the mixture was too much for me. I threw one last handful of stones at the water and stamped off through the dark, leaving the others to make their own way home.

It was hard finding the place where the path met the beach, and still harder not to wander off it on the way up to the house. Behind me were thrashing noises and a voice chanting:

"Although I joy in thee,
I have no joy of this contract tonight.

It is too rash, too unadvis'd, too sudden – Ouch! Damn!"

I hurried because I had had enough of Juliet, to say nothing of Alice. If I'd had the choice at that moment between a cheeseburger and an hour of solitude, as much as I missed junk food, I would have chosen the solitude. Unfortunately, I didn't have the choice because somebody screamed.

I turned around and sped back down the path again faster than I'd ever taken it in daytime. If I had run into a hornets' nest that night, I don't think I would have noticed. I hardly even noticed bumping into Alice, and Alice was so worried herself that she forgot to object.

"That was Minnow!" she gasped.

We stumbled the rest of the way down to the beach together and found Minnow crouched behind a driftwood log, shaking with sobs.

Alice ran up and threw her arms around her. "What are you hiding for? Why did you scream?"

Minnow pointed at the water. "Murdering thieves!" she whispered.

I peered out at the bay and caught my breath. A man's head stuck out of the water, staring at us with bulging eyes. He was bald, with a shiny black scalp and a mustache.

I clutched Alice, then laughed. "It's only a seal, Minnow. I never saw one come so close before."

The seal must not have liked being laughed at, because he ducked his head under and vanished. Alice tossed a stone, but all that happened was a pool of phosphorescence.

Alice went first up the path this time, and I followed, holding Minnow's hand.

"From now on, we don't lose sight of each other for one second," I announced.

"Not even to go to the bathroom?" asked Minnow.

"Not even," I said firmly. "And you can sleep in my bed tonight. Why didn't you leave the beach with Alice? Every time you stray off, something scary happens."

"I *meant* to go with Alice," Minnow explained, "but I kept wanting to throw one more stone, and when I was ready, she was already gone, and that man was there instead. I didn't dare shout for help because I thought he'd shoot me."

"Serves you right," I said, but I squeezed her hand.

Alice put on the kettle, and we had tea with lots of sugar in it before going to bed. I let Minnow sleep with me as I promised, but first I made her brush her teeth and say her prayers.

Usually, Minnow says "Now I Lay Me Down to Sleep," but that night, she chose an old Scottish prayer that's my mother's favorite:

"From ghoulies and ghosties and long-leggety beasties
And things that go bump in the night,
Good Lord, deliver us!"

"You said a mouthful!" I told her as I turned off the light.

I heard a loud bump in the night as Alice let her book slide to the floor. For once, she didn't insist on reading herself to sleep. She murmured,

"Three words, dear Romeo, and good night indeed.
If that thy bent of love be honorable,
Thy purpose marriage, send me word tomorrow . . ."

Then she yawned and shut up.

I gave a silent prayer of thanks that we were all safe and sound in one room: Minnow and Alice and Juliet and me.

CHAPTER EIGHT

I don't know how it happened, but I woke up on the floor. Somehow, Minnow must have wedged her feet against my stomach again and shoved me right out of that bed. I felt cold and bruised, and it didn't help when Minnow sat up all flushed from a comfortable night's sleep and asked, "What are you doing down there, Allegra – exercises?"

"Feel free to move back to your own bed now," I told her sarcastically.

"No, thanks," said Minnow. "It's morning. Do you think Mummy and Daddy will come on the early boat?"

I stood up stiffly and pulled on a pair of wool socks. "Of course not! It takes four and a half hours to drive up from Boston. If they wanted to make the early boat, they would have had to get up before dawn. They'll probably try for the one-thirty."

"They'll take the four-twenty," Alice mumbled sleepily from

the other bed. "For once, they don't have us in the car. They can stop for those expensive lobster rolls on the way."

Minnow picked up the alarm clock and wrinkled her brow. "But maybe they wanted to get up early, so they'd better get to Rockland in exactly one hour, or they'll lose their reservation."

"Pooh!" said Alice. "They're sitting in the kitchen having coffee, and Daddy just burned the toast, and Mummy's pretending she doesn't mind, but he can tell she's really furious."

I laughed. Alice's description was perfect except for one thing: I couldn't help seeing them both worried to death and as if they hadn't slept all night. I imagined them waiting for the phone to ring.

An idea came to me suddenly. Since they were coming back that day anyway, there was no harm in their knowing where we were, so long as they didn't find out we had been there all the time. "Guess what?" I said. "We were on that early boat!"

I raced downstairs, snatched up the telephone receiver, and dialed our number in Boston. This time, my mother answered. "Mummy?" I said. "Hi! It's me, Allegra."

The voice at the other end of the line sounded cross but not too worried. "Allegra? What on earth – "

"I can't talk," I said quickly. "We're in Rockland, and Aunt Ruth wants to take us to a place for breakfast. We have to catch the early boat, but don't worry, we'll walk home – "

My mother broke in angrily. "We called and called! Put Aunt Ruth on the phone, Allegra."

"She's in the ladies' room," I told her. "See you this afternoon!" and I hung up the receiver.

Minnow had followed me downstairs. She gazed at me in awe, mixed with disapproval. "Allegra! That really was a lie!"

I sighed. "At least they know we're on the island – or almost, if we were really on the early boat – and they won't drive to Belfast. And maybe they'll believe us! I mean, why be pessimistic? With luck, they'll never mention the subject when Aunt Ruth's around, and..."

The disapproval in Minnow's face turned to disbelief. I gave up and sent her out to pick raspberries for breakfast while I mixed up some pancake batter.

The sun and heat the day before had done wonders for the bushes around our house. Minnow picked a whole bowlful of berries, and we folded them into the batter. Typically, Alice didn't get herself downstairs until the food was on the table. We could hear her taking the steps slowly as she recited in a solemn voice:

"*What's here? a cup, clos'd in my true love's hand?*"

Thump!

"*Poison, I see, hath been his timeless end.*" Thump!

"Something smells good, Legs!"

"Why don't you come down early and make your own poison for once?" I asked sourly as I held out a plate of pancakes.

"I will tomorrow," Alice promised, taking six. She eats like a pig. It's a wonder she stays so slim and poetic-looking.

"That's a big help! Tomorrow, Mummy will be here to cook. They're coming this afternoon, remember?"

"Yes, and you know what?" Minnow added excitedly. "Allegra called while you were still in bed and told them Aunt Ruth was putting us on the early boat from Rockland!"

Alice chewed noisily while she thought this over. Then she swallowed, pushed her chair back from the table, and stood up. "That doesn't give us much time, does it!"

"Time for what?" I asked.

"To find the treasure," said Minnow. "It's got to be outside, Allegra. That's the only place left it could be. Let's all go out and dig."

Alice shook her head. "I mean time to clean up, dummy! If we didn't get back until this morning, why would the house be looking like this?"

Alice so seldom comes up with anything practical that when she does, it knocks me for a loop. She was absolutely right; the house was in a week's worth of mess.

In the beginning, we had made our beds and washed up after meals, but somehow, as the days passed, we were too busy to keep it up. First, the beds went. It seemed senseless to make them in the morning just to unmake them again at night, with no parents to inspect them in between. Then we let the dishes pile up in the sink and only washed the ones we needed when we ran out.

We hadn't used the oven, but the stove burners were full of charred crumbs and grease, and there was flour all over the kitchen floor, to say nothing of the dirt we had tracked in from outside. Books and magazines were scattered around wherever the reader had thought was a good place to read. We hadn't done any laundry, so our dirty clothes were scattered around, too. What's more, the whole house smelled of low tide due to the pile of mussel shells outside the kitchen door, and the lawn needed mowing.

"Let's forget the lawn," I said. "If we hadn't been here, it would have grown just the same. Let's start with the kitchen."

Alice washed the dishes while I scrubbed the burners and Minnow swept the floor. Then I took the vacuum into the living room and sent my sisters upstairs to make their beds.

"Pick up all your dirty laundry and put it in the basket, okay?" I yelled after them. "And make my bed, too, will you, Alice? When I get through down here, I'll clean the bathroom."

I regretted my words when I saw the tub. Only Alice had bothered taking baths, but she had made up for the rest of us by taking two a day. She had been generous with my mother's bath salts, and unfortunately, they weren't the kind that don't leave a ring. In short, the tub was disgusting. I was feeling really sorry for myself by the time I finished and went to see how Minnow was getting along.

Minnow is hardly an expert at bedmaking. I could see I would have to do hers over again myself. There were shells and empty bottles of school glue all over the room. Minnow was sitting in the middle of the floor, surrounded by a whole drawerful of underpants.

"What on earth are you doing?" I asked.

"Counting," said Minnow. "Mummy says to change my socks and underpants every day. She'll get mad if there aren't seven dirty pairs of each."

"But you're counting clean ones!" I protested.

"I know," said Minnow. "I can only find one dirty pair."

"Don't tell me you wore the same ones all week!" I said as I saw her choose six clean pairs to add to the dirty one.

Minnow glared at me. "Of course not, stupid! I just misplaced a few, that's all."

"You lost six pairs of underpants?" I asked.

"One went out to sea, remember?" Minnow reminded me. "And one pair stayed on the picnic beach, and the others I just can't find."

I found a pair in her bed while I was remaking it, and another inside some dirty jeans. What happened to the rest remained a dark mystery. I know it wasn't really important, but I felt madder and madder, and more and more self-righteous, as I searched through the mess in Minnow's room for those underpants.

"One thing is for sure," I said as I groped under the bed. "I'll never have kids of my own when I grow up. Looking after you and Alice for seven days has been enough for a lifetime."

Minnow slipped her thumb into her mouth for the third time that week.

"Hey, what's this?" I cried, pulling out a dusty wisp of blue-flowered nylon. "Eureka! Only three to go."

Minnow took one look and said, "Those aren't mine. They're Alice's."

"Then what, may I ask, are they doing under your bed?" I held them at arm's length, shook them, and turned to march indignantly out of the room, only to bump into Alice, who was leaning against the door.

"Guess what, Allegra?" Alice drawled. "I happen to *keep* my dirty underpants under Minnow's bed. That's where they belong, so would you mind putting them back?"

My jaw dropped, and Alice laughed. "Oh, fuss, fuss, fuss! You're always fussing if things aren't exactly the way you think they should be."

"That's right," said Minnow, suddenly sticking up for her rights. "You're bossy! You've been bossing us around all week."

"But now Mummy and Daddy are coming home, so you can give us a break," Alice added. "Why don't you relax and just have fun? This whole week was supposed to be fun, remember? But all you've done is fuss, fuss, fuss!"

I was speechless. My sisters almost never gang up on me. We just don't do that in our family. Besides, I couldn't believe their ingratitude. Who had lain awake worrying every night? Who had done all the cooking and made all the plans and kept those two nuts from killing themselves? And they called it fuss!

I felt deflated, like an old balloon. Nothing seemed special anymore, even though I was in Maine.

"Sorry," I said. "I didn't mean to be bossy. It was a stupid idea anyway, to stay here. We would have been better off with Aunt Ruth."

I guess that didn't sound like me. Usually I get mad, but I felt so depressed that I didn't have the energy to defend myself. For one terrible moment, it occurred to me that maybe I was the dumb one, and only my sisters knew what life was all about. I began to cry.

Then suddenly, everything was all right again. Minnow hugged me, and Alice moved closer so that her shoulder was touching mine.

"I would have died if I had had to spend this week with Aunt Ruth," said Alice. "You saved my life, Legs!"

"You put soda on my stings," said Minnow.

"We might have died even *here*, without you," Alice continued. "You're the one who found out what was safe to eat. And even if it wasn't awfully good, it kept us alive."

"And you cooked it," said Minnow, "and then you held my head when I was sick."

Enough is enough. I wiped my tears. "You know perfectly well it wasn't my cooking that made you sick, Minnow! You were sick because you made such a pig of yourself with Alice's pepperoni."

I felt a little ashamed, so I changed the subject. "You know what? We ought to do something special to welcome Mummy and Daddy back. How about if we have a feast ready for them when they come home? Especially since they won't be able to have a gin and tonic after that hot drive."

"Especially since we never found the treasure," Minnow added.

"Daddy always buys a bottle in Rockland before he takes the ferry, anyway," Alice reminded me.

"We'll keep it simple, but we'll make it really nutritious," I said. "That way, if they've already found out we were here all week, at least they'll see we knew how to take care of ourselves."

Alice and Minnow looked dubious, but they sat down and helped me plan the menu.

First, we decorated the table. Alice put down our best cloth, and Minnow picked a bunch of black-eyed Susans for the centerpiece. We went to the woods to gather chanterelles and down to the shore for orach to make a salad. I mixed up some batter for raspberry pancakes, but I put the bowl aside for later.

"Now all we need are periwinkles," I said. "Let's see if the tide is low enough. Anyway, I could do with a swim."

It was a hot, still day. Usually, on the island, you get a cool breeze. Sometimes, we're even wearing sweaters when the radio says the heat is stifling over on the mainland. But not that day. The sun beat down on our backs and glared up from the rocks. There wasn't a ripple on the bay. Luckily, the water is chilly even on the hottest days, so after filling our bucket with periwinkles, we dunked.

"Now I'm cold again!" Alice complained. She was lying at the edge of the beach and resting her chin on a stone, like a crocodile.

"Your lips are purple," I told her. "Are mine, too?"

"*I will kiss thy lips,*" Alice quoted ghoulishly. "*Haply some poison yet cloth hang on them –* "

"Oh, no, you don't!" I shouted, and I shoved her head underwater.

We paddled around for a long time, getting too cold in the water and then too hot again as we dried off. It was frustrating.

Suddenly, Minnow jumped up and squeaked.

"What's wrong now?" I asked. "Did you step on a sea urchin?"

"The percolator!" she cried. "I left it up in my cupboard. I want Mummy to see it right away so she forgives us for staying here."

I had a suspicion that seeing her only percolator covered with shells and school glue might have the opposite effect on my mother, but I didn't want to hurt Minnow's feelings. I knew she wouldn't relax until her work of art had its proper place in the middle of our feast.

"Oh, get dressed and go back home, then," I said. "But don't mess anything up. Take these periwinkles while you're at it. And you know what you could do while you're up there?"

"What?" Minnow asked suspiciously.

"There's a big pile of mussel shells outside the kitchen door," I told her. "We couldn't possibly have eaten that many in half a day. Get rid of them, will you?"

After Minnow left, Alice and I stayed at the beach for a while, baking in the sun, cooling off in the water, and talking.

"Did you notice the trash when we were cleaning up?" I asked.

Alice's front had steamed dry. Now she turned around to dry her back. "No. What about it?"

"There wasn't any," I informed her. "When Mummy and Daddy are here, we drive to the dump twice a week. But the whole time we were here alone, there was only the marmalade jar and the cracker box and a few tea bags. It shows we haven't been eating a lot of junk food with plastic wrappers and stuff. Except for your pepperoni, that is."

"Pepperoni isn't junk food," Alice argued. "The kind I get comes wrapped in its own skin, and you eat that, too. It's a lot better for you than all that penny candy you keep buying at Waterman's."

I must admit I have a passion for penny candy. It's so much fun to choose, and you get such a lot for your money.

"I can't wait to get back to Waterman's!" I said. "I'm going to buy four licorice shoestrings, two of those caramels with the white swirl – "

"The caramels aren't worth it," Alice interrupted. "They don't last long enough."

"That's why I'm only getting two," I explained. "Then I'll get six lemon drops, two – "

I never reached the end of my list because Minnow came tearing down the path to the beach, screaming her head off.

"I knew it!" I told Alice. "I *knew* we couldn't get through the last day without another disaster. What do you think it is this time?"

"More bees?" Alice suggested.

But it wasn't bees. "Murdering thieves!" Minnow screamed. "Help! Murdering thieves!"

I groaned. "Oh, Minnow. Grow up!"

"It's true, Allegra," she said, panting. "There was one in the house, and I caught him!"

"*You* caught a murdering thief?" asked Alice. "How did you do it? What happened?"

We got Minnow's story in little squeaks and gasps. Apparently, she had been upstairs in her room when she heard someone coming up the driveway. By the time she got the shutter open all she could see was a bicycle out on the lawn. She was terrified, but she preferred making a dash for the beach to hiding under the bed and waiting to be murdered. She tiptoed downstairs, and on her way through the kitchen, she heard someone bumping around in the storeroom.

"So you turned around and ran?" I guessed.

"Of course I didn't!" said Minnow indignantly. "What if that thief ate our feast? What if he stole my percolator? I slammed the storeroom door on him and locked it. Look, here's the key!"

"If all that's true, Minnow, you're the bravest person in the world!" I said, giving her a hug. "Who on earth do you think it is?"

"I *told* you! It's a thief!" said Minnow. "He was after the treasure. It's a good thing I found it first."

"It's a good thing you *what*?" I shrieked. "What do you mean, you found the treasure? Where is it?"

There was a slight bulge in Minnow's T-shirt, just above where she had tucked it into her jeans. Stretching the neck, she reached inside and pulled out a rectangular bundle wrapped in a dusty flannel cloth. Alice and I both grabbed at it, but Minnow held it back.

"No, you don't!" she said. "I found it. I don't mind sharing, but I get to open it first."

"But where was it, Minnow?" asked Alice.

Minnow's cheeks were flushed with pride. "It was in my cupboard, the one that's built right into the wall, remember? I kept the percolator on the bottom shelf, and when I took it out, some of the shells fell off, and – "

"Oh, get to the point," I said impatiently.

Minnow glared at me. "This *is* the point! One of the shells fell through a crack, and it sounded like there was a big space down there where it fell. Then I noticed the bottom shelf was wobbly, so I pried it up with my comb, and I found a whole lot of dead flies and this!"

The flannel cloth was frayed and faded, and looked very old. Minnow unfolded it reverently, only to find a second layer of cloth – it looked like a man's handkerchief – tied with cotton tape. I was itching to tear the tape off any old way to see what was inside, but Minnow unpicked the knot, holding her breath the way she does on Christmas morning.

"What is it? Hurry, what is it?" I cried, and Alice started to gnaw at a fingernail.

When Minnow finally got the knot undone and pulled off the second layer of cloth, I was so disappointed I thought I'd burst into tears. It was nothing but a pack of letters.

Alice was the first to speak. "Never mind, Minnow. It isn't your fault. At least now we know all those wall cupboards might have false bottoms. We can go back home and look in the others."

Minnow shook her head violently. "I'm not going up there again. I'm scared of the thief."

Alice brightened. "I forgot about the thief. He proves there's really something hidden in our house, doesn't he? Should we call the police?"

"There's only a summer constable that I know of," I said. "I wouldn't know how to get hold of him."

"Let's go ask the neighbors," Minnow suggested.

We don't really have any neighbors. What Minnow meant was some summer people who live about two miles away, once you get out on the main road.

"They aren't coming until August this year," I said. "Anyway, they don't have a phone."

We crept cautiously toward the house. Thieves are supposed to have skeleton keys, so maybe this one could unlock the storeroom door from the inside and escape. We were afraid he was lying in wait for us, but the bicycle was still on the lawn, and as we neared the house, we heard a lot of thumping and yelling.

"You know something?" I said. "It sounds more like a woman than a man."

We all listened. There was no doubt about it: It was a woman's voice shouting.

"Women thieves!" said Alice in a shocked tone. "What next?"

"Oh, don't be so old-fashioned!" I told her. "I bet women would make better thieves than men, even. I have a plan. You stay here with Calvin Moon's axe. It's over there by the woodpile. Minnow and I will flag down a car out on the main road. If the thief tries to come out of the house, just clobber him."

"Gee, thanks!" said Alice. "But I have an even better plan. *You* stay, and *I'll* flag down the car."

"There's a car coming right now," said Minnow.

We stopped talking and turned toward the driveway.

"Accomplices!" whispered Alice. "Let's hide!"

It was too late to hide. A shabby blue station wagon drove around the corner. It was *our* station wagon, with our parents in it. They must have started right after my phone call and caught the one-thirty boat.

The three of us stood frozen to the ground. For a brief, cowardly moment, I wished we had spent the week with Aunt Ruth after all.

Then my father climbed out of the car and waved. The gesture must have reassured Minnow because she squealed and ran toward him with her arms stretched out.

"Daddy! Daddy!" she shouted happily. "Welcome home! We used up all the gin, but there's still some vodka left!"

CHAPTER NINE

Luckily, my father didn't seem to register what Minnow said about the gin. He was too busy hugging us to ask questions, and when the hugs were over, he was too busy helping my mother unload the supplies.

As for my mother, she struggled out of the car laden with grocery bags, a long-handled mop, and a stack of flowerpots. "It's been impossible to get hold of you!" she gasped. "Why didn't you warn us that you were leaving for Quebec?"

Alice and Minnow looked to me for the answer. I hedged. "How did you find out about Quebec?"

"One of Aunt Ruth's neighbors told us," said my father. "We called her when we couldn't get through to you. She said, 'They've gone to Quebec.'"

"Why on earth Aunt Ruth would want to drag you three monkeys all the way to Quebec and back, I can't imagine," my mother added. "I know she's the most reliable person in the world, but it's unlike her not to have let us know. For a moment there, we were in a panic."

"Besides," my father added, "she must have gone to considerable expense. As soon as she tells me how much it amounts to, I'll mail her a check. Did you stay in a hotel?"

Again my sisters looked at me reproachfully, with their mouths clamped shut. It was obvious that within a day or two, my parents would be talking with Aunt Ruth anyway, so I took a deep breath and confessed.

"When the neighbor said 'they,' she must have meant Mrs. Pitts, not us. We never went to Aunt Ruth's. We stayed right here."

"Right here on the island?" My mother dropped the flower-pots and turned pale. "All week by yourselves?"

"Relax!" my father said, patting her on the shoulder. "They're safe, and there are three of them – count for yourself. We can find out what happened as soon as we have the groceries put away. I'm afraid the frozen stuff will melt. Get Dickie Moon to come out and help us, will you, Allegra? Ask her, don't tell her, or she'll take offense."

"Dickie Moon?" I echoed. "She isn't here."

"Then what's her bicycle doing on our lawn?" my father asked.

He moved toward the house, but Minnow screamed, "Don't go inside, Daddy! There's a murdering thief in there."

My father stared at Minnow with an amused look on his face. "A murdering thief, Minnow? What do you mean?"

"I caught one!" said Minnow. "I heard him looking for the treasure, so I locked him in the storeroom. Here's the key."

"Except it's not a him," said Alice. "It sounds more like a her."

"Thief?" my mother repeated, looking dazed. "Treasure? What on earth are you girls talking about?"

I looked from Minnow to the bicycle and back to Minnow again. "You know what, Minnow? I think maybe you made a mistake. It was Dickie Moon that you locked in the storeroom, and she's going to be hopping mad!"

For a moment, I thought my father would explode. His mouth twitched, and he snorted, and there was a dangerous gleam in his eyes. Then he burst into laughter.

"Hand over that key, Minnow," he said. "I can see you've had enough emotion for today. I'll go beard the lion in her den."

Dickie Moon took offense, to put it mildly. The problem was, she thought *we* were murdering thieves. Apparently, Calvin had been lobstering the night before and saw a light. Dickie had come by to check it out. But she never got any farther than the storeroom because Minnow locked her up.

"I'm sorry, Dickie," said Minnow. "If I'd known it was you, I never would have done it."

"You must have recognized my voice," Dickie grumbled.

"I ran away before you started shouting," Minnow explained. "And afterward, we didn't dare go into the house in case you got out. We thought you were after the diamonds."

Instead of making things better, that made them worse. Dickie blushed and tears came to her eyes. "You folks don't have any diamonds that I've seen, and I'm not the type to steal them if you did."

It took my parents a long time to calm her down and explain all over again that we thought it was murdering thieves, not Dickie Moon, after the diamonds. Which we didn't have in the first place. I don't think Dickie ever understood. She forgave us, but she grumbled the whole time she was unpacking the groceries, and she wasn't very nice about the percolator.

"I don't know what those kids have been up to," she told my mother, "but that thing is going to take a heap of cleaning."

"Cleaning!" Minnow wailed. "It's that way on purpose. It's a work of art!"

Dickie laughed. "Art? Them stinking shells?"

That did it. Minnow started to cry, and Alice scowled at Dickie and called her "serpent heart." Alice likes Dickie – we all do – but she can't stand for anyone to hurt Minnow's feelings.

My mother finally sent Dickie home. Then she told Minnow that the percolator was the most unusual shell project she had ever seen, in or out of a museum.

I have to hand it to my mother: She really has tact. Minnow cheered up right away. "I knew you'd be happy!" she said, wiping her nose on the back of her hand. "I'm just afraid it'll be hard to make coffee in it."

"I wouldn't *dream* of making coffee in it," said my mother. "I'm going to put it on the shelf where we can all admire it, and I'll buy another percolator at Waterman's tomorrow."

"Oh, can I go, too?" I asked. "I'm dying for some penny candy."

"I'm dying for anything store-bought," said Alice. "I'd even eat lima beans after what we've been swallowing all week." Alice despises lima beans.

"Me, too," said Minnow. "Survival stinks!"

"Survival?" my mother repeated. "What *have* you been eating? And what were you doing here in the first place? How did you get back from Rockland? And what on earth – "

My father walked into the kitchen and interrupted her. "Okay, kids," he said. "Let's have the whole story. And you'd better make it a good one, or there are going to be some sore bottoms this afternoon."

The last time one of us had been spanked was the summer Minnow was four and she let loose twelve pounds of live lobsters. We only buy lobsters once a summer as a special treat, but when we do, my father buys a lot. He says the only way to enjoy a special treat is to have too much so that it takes a whole year before you want more again. I agree with him. But Minnow felt so sorry for those lobsters that she snuck them down to the beach and let them all swim away.

Except for the lobster incident, my father isn't really a spanking person, but that day, I was afraid that no matter how good I made our story, we were in trouble. Still, it was worth a try.

"You see, Aunt Ruth called to say we couldn't come after all," I began. "She had to go visit a sick friend in Quebec, but we couldn't bear the idea of going back to Boston, so we never told you. When you drove off the ferry, we just stayed on and came back to the island."

"It took hours to walk home," Alice complained. "Allegra made us pack our suitcases so you wouldn't suspect anything. They weighed a ton."

"And there wasn't any food," Minnow piped up. "All week, Allegra made us eat survival!"

"Why don't you let Allegra speak for herself?" my father asked. "She seems to have been the ringleader in this escapade."

So I told the whole story from beginning to end, without leaving out a thing, not even Minnow being sick, and losing her underpants, and hiding from the seal. Not even the time Alice got trapped in the nude by that boat at the picnic beach.

My mother turned her back after a while. Her shoulders were shaking. My father was trying hard to keep a straight face, but some of the time he wasn't very successful. When I finished, however, he sobered up.

"What you haven't explained is why you did it in the first place," he said.

"I didn't want to miss even one minute of being on the island," I told him. "We weren't hurting anybody by coming back here and staying by ourselves. And I thought it would be fun to have a week of complete freedom."

We weren't spanked, but we got the scolding of our lives. I thought my father would never stop preaching, and my mother had a lot to add.

"It's the inconsideration that I mind the most," she said. "It turned out that no one knew, so no one worried. But what if we had tracked down Aunt Ruth and found out you weren't with her? Think how frightened we would have been!"

We kept saying that we were sorry and wouldn't dream of doing it again, but it took my parents a long time to wind down. Finally, my father shrugged. "I suppose you'll never really understand until you're parents yourselves."

"I've been a parent all week!" I protested.

My father stared at me with a teasing look in his eyes. "Perhaps you're right," he said. "Tell me, how did you enjoy complete freedom?"

"There wasn't any," I confessed. "It was all worrying about Minnow and Alice, and worrying about food, and worrying about when the tide was low enough for mussels, and things like that. To say nothing of all that time we wasted hunting for treasure! We thought once we found it, everything would be all right. But then Minnow *did* find it, and it turned out to be nothing after all. If it really was the treasure, I mean."

When I ran out of breath, my mother smiled. "What are you talking about? Did Minnow really find something?"

I sighed. "Only a bunch of old letters. But we found out the wall cupboards have false bottoms, so maybe there's something in one of the others."

My father's eyebrows shot up. "Letters?" he repeated, his voice rising about two octaves in his excitement. "Did you say old letters? Where are they? Show them to me!"

For the second time, Minnow reached inside her T-shirt and pulled out the flannel-wrapped bundle. My father snatched it away from her and tore off the layers of cloth with trembling hands.

"They found them!" he shouted, and his face was just like Minnow's when she's excited. "*They found those letters! Fantastic! Stupendous!*"

"Minnow found them," I reminded him, "not us. What's so special about them? I thought we were looking for diamonds, or at least gold coins."

My father laughed and calmed down a little. "This is a heck of a lot better than diamonds, to me, anyway, and I can name a bunch of other people who would give their eyeteeth for them. Do you have any idea what they are? Did you look at them?"

We shook our heads.

"They're written by Henry Wadsworth Longfellow, that's all!" my father crowed. "They're what your uncle Benjie was hinting about all that time. Longfellow wrote them a hundred and fifty years ago to your Great-great-grandfather Benjamin Sloane. If they don't make my career, I'll eat my hat!"

Minnow was unimpressed. "I've never tasted a hat, but I bet it's not as bad as survival."

My father slipped Longfellow's letters into his inside jacket pocket and patted them affectionately. "How do you go about eating survival, Minnow? And what is it, by the way?"

"That," I said, pointing to the table. "We tried a lot of other stuff as well, but most of it wasn't very appetizing. It was a real pain to prepare, too."

"Served you right," said my mother. "But I guess you've earned a vacation from the kitchen. I'll take over the meals for a while."

"You won't have to today," said my father, "not with a feast like this waiting for us."

I felt really proud, but Alice and Minnow looked glum. "I'm sick of survival!" said Minnow. "Couldn't Mummy and Daddy eat survival and the rest of us have hot dogs?"

My mother laughed. "How about roast beef? And there's corn on the cob, and ice cream for dessert."

It seemed strange to be sitting on the beach that afternoon while my parents stayed home and cooked the roast. Every time I began to relax, I'd forget and start worrying about where our next meal was coming from. Old habits die hard.

"What should we do?" I asked my sisters. "It doesn't feel right, just doing nothing."

"It feels good to *me*," said Alice. She lay back and shut her eyes.

It was high tide, and the water licked in and out of the round rocks at the top of the beach. There was a salt smell mixed with the smell of wild bay leaves. The sun glinted on the red and orange lobster buoys, bobbing out in the deep water. Minnow threw a stone at one, startling a loon, who gave us an offended look and swam away, hooting.

As I looked out over the bay, all sorts of thoughts tumbled around in my head. What if those letters from Longfellow to Great-great grandfather Benjamin Sloane did more than make my father's career? What if they made his fortune? What if they were worth so much money that he didn't need to rent the house to strangers in August and we could stay in North Haven all summer? What if he got so rich he didn't have to teach any-more, and we could stay all year? Would I go to school on the island? Could we afford to keep our own sailboat?

Suddenly, a horsefly stung me on the shoulder. I stopped daydreaming and flapped my arms to discourage him from trying it again.

"Maine would be perfect without the horseflies," I said as I scratched the red welt he left on my skin.

"And bees, and barnacles," Minnow added.

Alice laughed. "They probably think Maine would be perfect without *us*."

"Actually," I said, "Maine *is* perfect, no 'withouts' about it. I love it more than any other place in the world! Don't you, Alice?"

Alice clasped her hands to her throat, rolled her eyes, and moaned:

"They are but beggars that can count their worth;
But my true love is grown to such excess
I cannot sum up half my sum of wealth."

Somehow that spoiled my mood. "Oh, for heaven's sake!" I snapped. "If you had any idea how dumb you look, you'd stop doing that. Unless Juliet had a voice like a duck and a pimple on her chin and a million mosquito bites, you couldn't be more unlike her."

Alice turned toward me with vengeance in her eye, but be-fore she could say anything, Minnow piped up. "Well, I'm *glad* Alice isn't like Juliet because if you ask me, Juliet was a nerd!"

I giggled, but Alice tried to keep her dignity. "We can't all be intellectuals," she told me haughtily. "But never mind, Allegra. I suppose the world needs a few fussbudgets, too, like horseflies, for the balance of nature."

"Who's fussing?" I asked. "I couldn't be more relaxed. Just think – we're on the island, and we don't have a worry in the world."

Minnow eyed me suspiciously. "That's exactly what you said a week ago, Allegra, and look what happened!"

A Note on the Type

The Worry Week has been set in Kepler, a multiple-master typeface designed by Robert Slimbach for Adobe in 1996. Rooted in the so-called modern types of the late eighteenth century, Kepler was designed to be free of the coldness and formality of its forebears while capitalizing on their refined appearance. Its multiple-master features endow it with the flexibility needed to serve a wide variety of typographic purposes and styles.

Design and composition by Carl W. Scarbrough